THE START OF YOUR NEW LIFE

A collection of 14 short stories

Ella-Jane Hobson

Copyright © 2023 Ella-Jane Hobson

All rights reserved

The characters and events portrayed in this book are fictitious. Any similarity to real persons, living or dead, is coincidental and not intended by the author.

No part of this book may be reproduced, or stored in a retrieval system, or transmitted in any form or by any means, electronic, mechanical, photocopying, recording, or otherwise, without express written permission of the publisher.

Cover design by: Ella-Jane Hobson

CONTENTS

Title Page
Copyright
The start of your new life   1
The final séance   5
A tentative deal   15
A single rose   29
Spacewalk   34
Road trip   38
Lighthouse   52
An Heirloom   62
Then there was light   69
My new home   76
A slow extinction   87
2744   91
Banished   106
Mr & Mrs Adair   122
The end of your new life   128
Afterword   129

THE START OF YOUR NEW LIFE

You woke up that morning, alarm blaring into your eardrum after falling asleep with it beside your bed. You'd been waiting on the message and staring so intently at the screen, mere inches away from your face. You could still feel the strain it had caused your eyes.

The message must have arrived moments after you fell asleep. We said it would, you tried your best to prove us wrong, but you missed the point. You thought we were implying you wouldn't care enough to stay up that late, or maybe even took it as a personal offence that you were too weak to be able to manage it, but you were wrong.

We were watching you.

Monitoring you, even.

We were waiting for you just as much as you were waiting for us. It wasn't a test like you believed. It was a show of power, of control, of how out of your element you were. And you missed it.

You were so excited, so self-obsessed, you missed the flags. There were plenty of them. Sometimes it seemed like you wilfully turned away from them, like you saw them and just chose to ignore them.

We liked that about you. So many potential candidates saw what you couldn't, it was unfortunate really. If they'd have turned a blind eye, they'd be here with us now.

Don't worry, though, we compensated their family. We're not monsters, after all. We'll compensate your family as well, maybe even your friends if you continue to progress.

You went out on a limb and we're proud of you. You dropped your life at a single message, suitcase in hand you headed to the station and left everything you knew behind. That was brave. Stupid, but brave.

We'd been watching you for a while. It's protocol to see what someone's like before reaching out. We can't go contacting any old person, the disappearances that could cause would lead to suspicion. We just can't risk it.

So we watch.

And we wait.

And if we think you've got what it takes, we reach out. Some of the people are awful, like genuinely bad. We don't feel so guilty disappearing those kinds of folks, honestly the world's a better place without them. Sometimes we reach out knowing they'll fail, to make up for all the hurt we cause. It's a little thing but it's a moment of reprieve for us.

You weren't like that though. We grew rather fond of you. We hope you do well, we hope you pass the test and make it out the other side. We don't want to disappear you.

You'd be missed. Your voice, your actions, your soul, all of you. You make the world a brighter place and for that we are truly sorry. We don't like it when people like you fail, it hurts us, makes this job a bit harder each time.

See, we don't just watch you, we watch the people around you as well, especially those you interact with regularly. We watch all the people you've cheered up, those who you've supported and understood and held space for even when it wasn't necessary. We watched the times you made someone laugh or cry or relax into your arms after a hard day and all they wanted was to feel loved.

They'll miss you so much. We know you won't believe that, and understandably so, but it's true. They valued you more than you realised, more than they realised, even.

One of your friends is here as well, it worked out so conveniently. You both walked away from your lives at such similar times. It'll make the cover story so easy. You were already so close. It'll be so easily believable.

You know, if it's required that is.

I have high hopes in you. We all do. We think you're our best chance yet, which is surprising to be honest. You seemed so normal at first, we almost overlooked you. One small act sealed your fate. It makes us wonder how many potentials we've missed because they didn't have that same opportunity.

Sometimes we wonder if a protocol change is about due, we haven't updated with the tech quite as much as we could've recently. It's ever so easy to overlook the constant changes that are going on. We got complacent so maybe it's time for an upgrade, results will be more accurate, there'll be less losses and more opportunities...

I guess we have you to thank for that.

You've been ever so useful already, you haven't even done the bulk of the work yet, that'll come soon enough, and you've helped us exponentially. We're almost glad you can hear this.

Almost.

See, we have to run some tests now. You won't like this bit. We need you conscious. We need you aware. It's going to be tough. Your brain might get a bit scrambled. Some cognitive functions are going to be impaired for a while, hand eye coordination might get a bit screwed, fine motor skills might get a bit funky. We don't know to what extent yet. Best case scenario, you'll be back to normal by next week. Worst case scenario...

You know what? Let's not go there. There's no need for you to know. You deserve better. Ignorance is bliss, as they say.

And, like I said earlier, we have high hopes for you. Maybe you'll ace this. Maybe you'll come out the other side completely intact. Maybe you'll prove our predictions wrong and have no adverse side effects. We'd like that.

The test will begin soon. We should've kept this much shorter. We shouldn't have gotten so sentimental. We shouldn't have strayed away from the script.

Technically we're breaking protocol by doing this, by talking for so long, but you're worth the reprimand. We just didn't want you to be alone for so long. We believe in you. We believe you'll make it through this in one piece. You'll achieve such great things, we're sure.

Before we go, we just want you to know it's OK to be scared.

We were too.

THE FINAL SÉANCE

Valencia

The light faded from the room considerably quicker than the sun had deemed necessary. Anyone walking past outside would have just assumed someone had closed an impressively dark and heavy pair of curtains. As for the people inside, they knew better.

The curtains were light and danced slightly in a breeze that had no obvious source, not that anyone noticed that for their attention was focused elsewhere. There was a problem that needed to be solved fast and paying attention to anything outside their immediate circle seemed somewhat redundant. So, the curtains went unnoticed, along with the shadows that crept just outside of the reach of the single candle that remained lit.

The candle had been placed intentionally in the middle of the only table in the room, which had been placed equally intentionally in the middle of the room.

It was nothing special, small, round, and decorative more than functional, at least for conventional purposes. Had someone thought to look at the underside, they would have noticed an intricate pattern carved into the wood that, to the untrained eye, would have been considered a pretty design far more worthy of somewhere visible. Anyone in the know would have understood.

I knew. That's why I brought it with me, specifically for the job I'd been called to. As soon as I had got the message, I dropped everything, only bringing the bare necessities. A few crystals, a mason jar full of salt, my favourite candle, all shoved haphazardly into my bag and balanced precariously on that table. It had been a bit of a drag carrying it to and from the train station, not to mention trying to get it through the various doors I had encountered on my journey, yet there were no chances of success without it and so I did what had to be done and annoyed many a pedestrian.

The trek was made in a hurry, only stopping briefly to retie my headscarf in an attempt to secure some of the flyway's off of my face, an attempt to look at least somewhat presentable before arriving. An attempt that was futile.

It wasn't until the front door opened and a gentleman looked down on me that I realised my mistake in looking so informal.

"Oh, you must be Valencia. If you would follow me, everyone's waiting."

I was used to that tone, disdain mixed with arrogance. My appearance had already proved him right, not that that was something that had ever bothered me. In fact it barely even crossed my mind as I followed him inside. People like him never took me seriously, but then people like him were never why I was there.

"You're finally here!" A lady exclaimed the moment she spotted me, though her face fell only moments later. "Damien, why didn't you help her carry her things through? That looks awfully heavy, here, let me help."

She rushed forward and took the closer half of the table. She let me lead and together we positioned it in the middle of the room.

"I cleared a space for you, just like you asked. I'm ever so sorry about Damien he's a science man and apparently devoid of manners. He thinks all of this is beneath him, I honestly didn't expect him to be quite so rude about it though."

"That's not a problem, Miss Katherine, right?"

"Call me Kitty."

"Miss Kitty. A lack of consideration is nothing compared to how some people have regarded me in the past. He's been adequately civil, all things considered."

"Well, that doesn't make it right. Damien, if you could go round up the others, I would be ever so grateful if we could get started sooner rather than later. After all, we can always chat once business has been sorted."

Damien left the room hurriedly, as if standing in my presence was the last place he wanted to be, or perhaps it was more to do with Kitty's admonishment of him. Either way, he soon found himself in the unfortunate position of standing in the unnaturally dark room, holding hands in a circle alongside the two people he had gone to find.

"There's a few things I want to make clear before we get started." I announced, once they'd settled into the positions I'd placed them in. "I can't guarantee that this is going to work, especially without co-operation. I need you all to be open and receptive and most of all, I need you to be calm and strong. Hold your place until I say it's safe not to. I need you all to promise me this, say it out loud."

There was a mixed chorus of "I promise." Some were clearly more meaningful than others. It didn't really matter though, a verbal contract had been made by everyone and that was all I needed.

A moment of silence went by, giving me a chance to survey the group in front of me. Kitty had insisted on standing on my left, perhaps slightly closer than was altogether necessary, but I had no desire to rectify that.

Beside her was Damien, visibly sceptical and bored, most likely on the lookout for any signs of a scam. And yet he stood there with the rest, he'd agreed freely to participate. The way he looked at Kitty provided me the more obvious reason, though I couldn't help but wonder if there was also an air of fear around him, as if the boredom and scepticism were covering something.

On his other side stood a girl, directly opposite me, the

second of the two that Damien had fetched. She was damn near the spitting image of Kitty, minus a few years and all of the enthusiasm of her sister. Now she was definitely scared, there was no mistaking that, and it didn't take long to figure out why.

Finally was the other of the two, a man whose curiosity was etched across his face and went by the name Claude. He was fascinated but oblivious. He had no idea what he was looking for, but he was clear on the fact that there was definitely something to be found.

The five of us stood around the table, watching the candle flame flicker while we waited for something to happen. Or more accurately, waited for something they could notice happening. Preferably something directly in front of them that fitted with their narrow idea of what was going on.

Fluttering curtains and creeping shadows didn't quite fit into that criteria for them, except for one. The girl that stood opposite me, she noticed but she refused to look anywhere besides my eyes. She was the only one that noticed the candle flicker and the wisp of smoke that drifted from it darkening. It left its casual upward route in favour of something far more directed.

"Nora, right?" I asked her, since I already held her gaze. She refused to reply, but she nodded so I continued. "You've been affected by this far more than the others, correct?"

Again she nodded but stayed silent as the shadows licked at her feet and a loose strand of hair fluttered gently across her cheek.

Kitty piped up on her behalf. "Nora, dear, was the first one to notice what was going on, she's also the only one to actually have seen the thing."

"You saw him? Is he the same one in here now?"

"Here? There's nothing in here!" Damien exclaimed, but no one paid him any attention, they were far too focused on Nora.

"Yes." Her voice was hoarse, as if she hadn't used it in weeks for anything other than screaming. "He's here."

"Do you know his name?"

She shook her head.

"Can you ask him?"

She shook her head again, though increasingly desperately.

"Nora, you're safe here. He can't hurt you."

"It's not safe." A door banged. "Nowhere is safe." Footsteps echoed. "He's going to hurt you."

"I know." I said it for her. I needed her to know that.

"Don't be ridiculous-" Damien started up again but Kitty cut him off.

"You know? Well, how did he know you'd be the one we'd call?"

"He knew it would be me because he made it so. Miss Kitty, you made the request, of course you would look for someone suitably empathetic for your dear sister, someone well versed in these matters, someone approachable and available as soon as possible. That narrows down who you can call pretty substantially. Especially that last part."

"Wait, what did you mean by I know?" Claude asked, speaking up for the first time since his introduction to me.

"Nora is an open door. It's through her that he arrived here, through her that he summoned me, and it's going to be through her that he tries to kill me."

Kitty gasped. "She would never do such a thing!"

"No, she wouldn't." I agreed sincerely. "For it wouldn't be her. Nora, dear, you're doing wonderfully. I need you to hold on for just a little bit longer. I'm also going to need you to tell me when you can't hold on any longer., is that something you can do for me?"

She nodded, substantially paler and sweatier than she had been only a few minutes before.

"Perfect. I won't ask for anything more than what you can offer. Right now, all he can do is pace around the perimeter of the room, he can't break through the salt circle quite yet. Soon enough he'll find his entrance and he won't hesitate. I don't know the specifics of how this will go down, but I know it's not going to be pleasant."

I directed all of this at Nora, she was the only one that needed to understand. "It's going to hurt. It's going to be scary. I want you to know that whatever happens here is not your fault, do you hear me? I know how this ends and it's not your fault."

"This is a load of nonsense." Damien declared, pulling his hand out of Kitty's. "Let go of me!"

"Valencia said-"

"I don't care! This is ridiculous and I have every right to leave this circus show whenever I deem fit!" He gestured wildly and uselessly.

"Cut it out. You made a promise. There's no use fighting it now."

"What have you done to us?" He asked, realisation dawning on him as he tried in vain to lift up his feet.

"You stepped into my circle and you made a promise. Now hush. Miss Kitty, Claude, I need my hands back for a moment. Actually, I assume Damien won't be joining in with the hand holding so perhaps we should forgo that aspect anyway."

"No! You listen here you witch, whatever you're playing at has to stop now-"

"You are in my domain now and you will listen to me. I am here to help these lovely young ladies deal with their problem, you can either let me do my job in peace, or I can make you."

"Make me? How could-"

I held up my hand and his words abruptly stopped while his mouth continued to form them. I watched him as his eyes grew wide and his anger subsided, obedience took its place.

"Good. Now, Nora, do I have your permission?" I asked as I removed the scarf from my hair. She nodded as I folded it a couple of times before walking over and gently tying it around her head, covering her eyes from view. "Thank you, and please tell me if it's uncomfortable."

She didn't say anything, didn't react in any way, so I just made my way back to my place in the circle.

"What's that for?" Kitty whispered unintentionally. She cleared her throat and tried again. "What's that for?"

"Us." I replied. "I can't make this any easier for her, I'm sorry, I wish I could. I can make it easier for us. Damien, Claude, you both have an important role to play. Keep her in place as best as you can. Between you, you're probably going to have to take most, probably all, of her weight, can you manage that?"

"We can do that." Claude confirmed.

"Kitty, watch her, where her eyes would be if they weren't covered. Blinking is fine but do not look away until I tell you. Promise me."

"I promise." She didn't hesitate. She'd seen Damien's consequences and she committed without a seconds thought regardless.

"Good. Nora, are you ready, dear?"

"Yes."

The candle flared, lighting the room up with bright, dancing, shadows cast across the group. Silence plummeted upon them, deafening silence that drummed through the ears and rattled the brain before being replaced by a high pitched humming noise that settled uncomfortably into the background.

Nora's body slumped and a window shattered. Damien and Claude dutifully held her up. They jumped at the sound but didn't react to the glass scattering across the floor, across the salt line. The dainty curtains did nothing to prevent it. He'd found his entrance.

I should have been more specific with them. "Keep her in place" was one thing when she was passed out, it was something else entirely once she was gone and he'd taken her place. They did good, nonetheless. They held her back long enough for me to place my chosen crystal in the fire of the candle. In turn, it held its place despite the battering it took from the smoke. It was playing her exact opposite.

Kitty held her gaze. She did a wonderful job, far better than I could have hoped. I wasn't sure it would work but Nora's head stayed firmly fixed on Kitty as she lunged at me.

I got halfway through the incantation before I felt a hand wrap around my rib. The chaos kicked back up instantly, every window rattled, several shattering from the pressure, the doors banged incessantly, and the sound of an army stomped all around us.

I don't know how long we stood there, Nora's head stuck facing Kitty, a sick smirk plastered on her face. He'd won. He'd reached inside me, he had achieved what he'd summoned me here for. I'd long since forgotten what my family had done to warrant such a vendetta, I was just one more death in a long and bloody history with him.

I accepted my fate. That was always the plan.

Until I heard Kitty's faint voice beside me.

She knew the words. She picked up where I had left off. She spoke what I could no longer say. And frankly her pronunciation was atrocious.

But it was more than good enough. She gave me time.

I grabbed the crystal from the fire, it had filled with smoke, filled with the love of Nora that the other's had for her. It was ready. I found her free hand, pressed it into her palm, and she screamed.

Kitty faltered. I still had a free hand so I sought hers out, I gently interwove my fingers with hers and, after a deep breath, she finished off the incantation.

Nora's scream froze, her body froze, the entire room froze. I smashed the crystal. Throwing it into the ground as hard as I could manage. The candle snuffed out. Nora dropped to the floor.

Silence fell. Not the loud kind. It was the silence of completion. It was soft, it was calm and peaceful. It was over.

Except for all the blood pooling at my feet. It dripped steadily out of my abdomen, the loudest thing in the room.

"Claude, carry Nora somewhere she can rest." I forced out. Most of it must have been legible for he did as I asked.

"Damien, fetch me some towels, I appear to be making quite a mess." He disappeared off into another room.

"Miss Kitty, I'm going to need my hand back, if that's alright?"

Her hand was still clutched in mine, though her grip was by far the stronger. She gasped an apology, hand flying towards her face, taking mine with it, before realising that was the exact opposite of what I'd asked. She let go and I lost a valuable source of warmth.

She hurried out of the room and rushed back in, dragging a chair behind her. She ushered me into it and I accepted gratefully.

"Where did you learn that?" I asked weakly.

"I couldn't hire someone to help us without doing some research first. There's an awful lot of disagreement amongst sources, but those words, they seemed to come up the most. I figured that meant they must have been important."

"How clever. The crystal pieces, wrap them in something, take it to a fast moving river, and throw it in. Sweep them up, do whatever, make sure you get it all. Doesn't matter if there's glass and debris in it, just make sure it's all there. I would normally..." I gestured vaguely at myself, I clearly wasn't in a fit state to be doing anything.

"Gather all the crystal, throw it into a fast river. Got it."

"Perfect. Tell her it wasn't her fault? I know she isn't to blame. I know she had no say in this. Tell her. She's going to need to hear it."

"You can tell her yourself-" I looked at her, properly looked at her. She couldn't finish that sentence any more than I could tell Nora what she needed to hear.

She tried a different approach instead, an easier one. "I'll send for my family's doctor, he's the best money can buy, he'll get you fixed up in no time and then we can go celebrate. I know a wonderful little joint just down on the square, I'm sure you'd love it there."

"That'd be swell."

A TENTATIVE DEAL

Henri

It was a tentative deal. One from higher up. We knew better than to ask. That didn't mean we didn't question it among ourselves, though.

If the sun was out, they were not to be disturbed. If we were moving on, we'd just leave them to catch up. Or vice versa, the sun would set and they'd scout the route ahead. Always the same group. Always the same deal. They took the night shifts. No negotiation.

It was hard not to speculate. It clearly wasn't an issue with seeing their faces or knowing them, they were great for a chat and a drink, sometimes even a full-on heart to heart when it was needed.

It wasn't a safety issue either, they were taking all the higher risk jobs, and coming back every time. 100% survival rate. There was no way the rest of us could've managed half the stuff they did.

Why waste the best on the mundane tasks we could fulfil, eh?

Most of the boys took it as a blessing. No one wanted to be walking around at night. It was bad enough during the day when you could actually see your feet and where you were putting them.

Suspicious lump up ahead? You can just step around it. Creepy rustle in the trees? A simple glance over there will show you whatever bird caused it. Can't do that at night.

That deal saved us more times than anyone cared to admit. The stories they came back with sometimes, about the planes, the ambushes, hell, sometimes even the locals. There's no way a group could get into that much trouble and not take any losses. In the early days we reasoned it was luck, but after a while we knew it had to be something more.

The first theory to spread, and probably the most believed theory, was super soldiers. Government experimentation that made those men more durable, more alert, more sensitive. Maybe the reason they could survive an ambush was because they knew they were walking into one. Maybe they could see in the dark, maybe they could even hear the enemies, maybe they were faster and stronger.

One of the boys swore down that they used echolocation. Claiming to have heard the tell-tale clicks and whistles coming from their end of the camp. We all laughed at that.

War was loud. Very loud. The kind of sensitivity needed for that was just unimaginable in such an environment. Improved hearing, sure, we could get behind that, but echolocation was a step too far.

Figured he just had bats on the brain. He had a book that he carried everywhere with three little bats doodled on the first page. Memento from his family back home.

Most of us had something similar. I had my girl's necklace. My mate had his kid's favourite doll. One of the night crew had this stunning antique ring, a family heirloom, handed down through each generation, apparently. The carvings on it resembled writing. I couldn't tell you the language, though I swear I could almost understand it. Like the knowing was right there, just a little out of my reach, but definitely there. I wasn't brave enough to ask about it. I wasn't brave enough to ask anyone about it.

Because, as friendly as they all were, as inviting and charming and every other sociable descriptor I could use, as much as all of those things were true, they scared me.

I remember when I first met them. As far as we knew they were just normal soldiers like the rest of us, and there's been times where I've almost believed they were. But there was something wrong about them. Something unsettling. I could've picked each one out of a crowd, but I couldn't have told you how or why.

I have since learnt my sentiments were shared, I wasn't alone in my paranoia. It probably wasn't even paranoia. As the super soldier rumours spread, so did everyone's first impressions of them. It was unanimous. The first few weeks were conflicting.

Most of us were pretty cold to them, myself included. Once we realised they were taking all of the undesirable jobs, we warmed up to them a bit. Inviting them for drinks was the least we could do, all things considered. That just spurred on the rumours though.

They were so open with us, and yet we never learnt anything about them. I was almost friends with one of them, Lucien, though I couldn't tell you anything about him. We had moments that felt intimate, we shared stories, we shared experiences, he understood things about me that no one else ever had, and I don't know how I know any of that.

Well, that's not entirely true.

We were moving camp, orders came and we were needed elsewhere so we packed up. It was daytime so we left them behind. That was standard by that point, we'd stopped questioning it, just upped and left knowing we'd meet them there. It was supposed to be easy. A walk through the countryside, take some supplies to a couple of villages that were on the way, get to the next camp by dinner time.

It started exactly as we expected, better even. The sun was up and people were happy to see us. We felt invincible. We were naïve.

The latter half of our journey wasn't as smooth. There'd been a lot of rain so everything was bogged down, getting the carts through the mud was challenging. It slowed us down greatly, and then a broken bridge across a burst river, it meant we arrived at the final village just as the sun was setting.

It was bright, it was blinding, distracting, and we were tired. The joviality of the morning had long since gone, swept down the river with one of the horses. We thought we were going to be welcomed. We thought we could relax. This was allied territory, after all. We were supposed to be safe.

We weren't quite that dumb though, thankfully. There was nobody around, no greeting, no hubbub of people existing like there should have been. We knew it was a bad sign, though maybe they just didn't recognise us, right? Strangers turning up ready for a fight, maybe they were just being cautious and staying hidden.

Me and bat boy went in first. Marcel. That was his name. Me and Marcel went in, we drew straws, lost fair and square so off we went.

There was a main road that ran through the heart of the village, we agreed it was probably the safest route to take, less enclosed, more sunlight, anything on the path would have been more visible. Less risk of ambush and whatnot.

We started out bored and moody. That changed as soon as we lost sight of our squad. It wasn't as quaint a village as we initially thought, much larger than the ones we'd stopped at earlier in the day. It made the emptiness much heavier.

Everything was clean. It wasn't an abandoned village, there was no chaos from running away, no signs of fighting, nothing had been left out of place. People clearly lived there, recently enough to keep it clean and tidied.

That's what I was thinking when we made it to the main square, this big open area surrounded by buildings. I pulled Marcel to a stop somewhere near the middle, somewhere we could see all around us.

I shared my concerns, he agreed. I thought we should go back, he disagreed. We had a job to do, we had to search the whole village and we hadn't even done half. He wouldn't leave the job partially done, so he picked a road and headed down. With or without me, he said.

I wasn't going to leave him so I followed. I let him lead us down the streets, he was careful about it, up until that one moment he wasn't.

There was a clatter. Something got knocked over and he wanted to investigate, it was fairly obvious which direction it had come from so we made our way towards it, slow and steady, guns up, stopping to listen, peering around corners, mentally preparing for an ambush but hoping for a civilian.

And there he was, a little kid, back up against the wall. We were still a little ways off but it was clear he was crying, sobbing even, hand over his mouth as his whole body shook.

Marcel lowered his gun, crouched down, arms open and inviting. He called out, "we're here to help", or something to that affect. The kid just looked at him, looked to the side, then an arm reached out and pulled him out of view as something clattered at our feet.

I didn't think. I kicked it away, kicked it towards where the kid had been only moments before. I grabbed Marcel and pulled him backwards and together we went flying.

I saw him hit the floor, saw his head... His eyes.... I saw the moment he... Left. I saw that damn book of his bounce off the floor and settle between us and then I saw nothing at all.

I was vaguely aware of a gun fight, somewhere in the not-so-far distance. It surrounded us but it didn't matter, nothing did. As far as I was concerned, we were both dead, my body just hadn't realised it yet.

At some point I opened my eyes. I didn't realise at first. I stared absently as my brain tried to piece together what was going on. The moon barely filtered down to me and there was just enough light to see someone crouching besides Marcel.

I wanted to ask for help. I didn't manage that. I did make a noise, though. The person turned to face me. He was holding

Marcel's wrist up to his mouth as his gaze locked onto mine. As he lowered the wrist and wiped his mouth, a name floated through my head. Lucien.

"He's gone."

I aimed for an affirmative noise, I think I managed it as he nodded and turned back to what he was doing. It felt intrusive to watch but I couldn't look away. I didn't think about what he was doing. I couldn't really think about much of anything. I could only wait. So that's what I did.

I waited until he was done. It took seconds. It took hours. Both of those statements were true but neither quite capture how long I was there for. Eventually he stood up.

I tried to do the same. I think I could have, given enough time, but it wasn't worth it. He let me try though, and I appreciated that, he waited until I gave up.

I think I muttered a weak "help". That was when he leant down and scooped me up like I didn't weigh a goddamn thing. I wasn't a small guy. He shouldn't have been able to do that. He shouldn't have been able to do a lot of things.

I didn't care though. Not at that point, at least. At that point I didn't care about anything, I just closed my eyes and drifted away to safety. Apparently a couple days passed before I woke up properly, a few of the boys in beds beside me.

They'd heard the explosion, realised what must have happened, and charged in. Well, stories differed in exactly how it all went down but the outcome was the same. I wasn't the only one to get carried out unconscious, almost half of us got hurt. Only three actual losses though, largely thanks to the night crew. They turned up right on time. Saved our asses. Saved the village as well.

A handful of Germans had taken over the place a week prior. Some traitors lived there, made it real easy for them, hid them from our scouts, planned and even set up that ambush.

The kid was fine. That's what Lucien told me. He came to visit regularly, even before I woke up. That's when we really became friends. Thinking back, we might have been sooner if I'd have been warmer to the idea. As it was, he didn't scare me anymore. Not in the same way, at least.

I didn't understand what I'd seen between him and Marcel. I knew it was an image I could never forget, but he'd saved me and that warranted my trust. So I gave it to him in abundance. I bared my soul to him. Shared it with him. That's what it felt like. That's what it feels like.

I'm not really sure how long I stayed in the med bay for. Far longer than I wanted. I was desperate to get back out there with the boys, but my entire left side was paralysed for what felt like days. I knew it was a temporary nuisance at most, but everyone else seemed to be concerned. They'd have sent me home then and there if they could, as it was, I got better and became useful again.

They couldn't afford to waste the man power, if I could walk then I could stay. Didn't even need to be all that good at it, apparently. Honestly, I suspect Lucien pulled some strings for me.

It took some practice but I figured out how to put one foot in front of the other again and gained a whole new respect for babies. But, hey, if they could do it then so could I.

It was great, hearing the cheers from my mates as I finally got out of bed for the first time, then to the end of the bed, to high five the guy staying across from me, to the door and almost back again. A little further each time I tried. There wasn't always an audience who cared, though it was better when there was.

Soon enough I was fit and ready for work. Or rather, stable enough to do simple tasks around the camp. There was plenty to be done so I was kept occupied, even if it wasn't quite what I wanted to be doing.

I was getting stronger, just waiting for the chance to get back out there. It was frustrating being camp-bound. I didn't really appreciate it until it put me exactly where I needed to be.

We had some last minute prepping to do, to send out a supply run. It was to leave at first light and I was tasked with final checks. Essentially, I had to read a bunch of labels and then stand around and make sure nothing got nicked while waiting for everyone to turn up.

The sound of voices was nothing unexpected, it was what I had been waiting for. I wasn't paying enough attention to recognise who it was until they came into view.

At some point I'd started looking out for Lucien. It wasn't a choice, more of an instinct, so when I realised it was the night crew the first thing I did was look for him. I scanned every face, two, three times. I caught their gaze and for some reason that brought them over.

"Everything alright, soldier?" The head of the group asked. I later learnt his name was Emile.

"Where is he? Lucien? You've never come back without him before?"

"The rumour mill is going to love this. It'll be the talk of the camp for months." One of them chimed in.

"We got into a skirmish. Couldn't afford to drag him back."

"He's dead?" I don't know what intonation there was in my voice, or maybe it was something on my face, either way the energy of the conversation changed. The way they regarded me turned to curiosity. I went from a comrade to a test subject.

"No. Injured. Probably not dead. Not yet. If he's not back by tomorrow, we'll revaluate that." He said it so casually but there was an intensity to him, and the rest of the group, that made me doubt it. I couldn't believe they'd be so apathetic about losing one of their own. I wouldn't believe that of anybody.

"Where?"

"Holed up in a shed somewhere. Piece of crap but sheltered and decently hidden."

"No. Specifically. Where?"

"What's it matter to you?"

"You might have your reasons to leave him behind but I don't."

"You're on duty, soldier."

"Switch someone out with me. You have the clearance, you can do that."

He looked me up and down. He should have argued, pulled rank and got me punished for my insolence. He didn't do any of that. I felt like a small child under his gaze. Somehow that was much worse.

Finally he turned away and I could be an adult again. "Alright then. Jules will go with you. He needs to be back in 20 minutes so make use of him while you can."

Jules stepped out of the pack and headed back the way they had come from, indicating for me to follow. As soon as I left my post, it got filled. I would have been reassured if I'd have cared. I had more important things on my mind.

We didn't talk. I just hobbled alongside him, trying my best not to slow him down. I thought I did a good job of it until I realised we must have been walking for almost fifteen of his twenty minutes. The realisation seemed to hit him at about the same time as me.

"This is as far as I can go, take the next left, you'll hit a bridge, don't cross it just follow the river downstream until you get to the fence, hop it and take... Hmm..." He glanced at my legs and took a moment to consider his next words, "Don't overthink it, take twelve paces, turn your back on the river and head amidst the trees. Keep going until you find a little shed. You'll know you're on the right track if you find the blood. Good luck."

He started to jog away before I could respond. I wanted to thank him. I spent too long thinking about it. He turned slightly and waved briefly before leaving my view. It almost felt like an acknowledgement of my thoughts.

I followed his instructions, grateful for how simple they were. Also how accurate they were, twelve paces was so specific. I tried not to overthink it. He was right though, my very inconsistent twelve paces got me where I needed.

I took the left, hit the bridge, followed the river, hopped the fence, well, fumbled over it, counted the twelve steps, and headed into the trees. The blood was painfully followable.

At first it was splatters, across the floor, the bark, the leaves, it gradually became puddles and then just one continuous smear. He didn't tell me the blood would be the track, a warning would have been appreciated.

The shed was more shrubbery than building, but it was where the smear lead so I assumed it was the right place. A rasping voice from the undergrowth confirmed it.

"Henri?"

"Lucien? You in there? Is there a door somewhere?"

"No door. Crouch." I obliged and spotted a hand. Pushing some ferns aside revealed a hole that was just big enough for me to crawl through. Once inside there was plenty of room, more so than it appeared from the outside. There was a door but it was very clearly and securely boarded up.

I stood up, wiped the blood off my hands, and started to ask about the door. Instead, I looked down at my friend and damn near threw up.

Turning to the wall for support, I just about managed to mutter, "I guess that explains all the blood."

He almost laughed. Maybe if his lung hadn't been hanging out of his side, he might have managed it. A huge chunk of his abdomen was just gone.

I sat down before I tried to talk any more. "What the fuck happened to you?"

"We got into a skirmish." He talked slowly. If I closed my eyes, I could almost imagine he was just half asleep with a bad headache. Something normal.

"That doesn't clarify a goddamn thing."

"Not at all, no. Why are you here?"

"You got into a skirmish."

"Touché."

"You saved me. Maybe I can repay the favour."

"How are you planning on doing that? Do you have some spare ribs I could borrow?" I gagged slightly at the thought, my hand instinctively hovering by my mouth. I stayed there a moment longer than needed, the image of him and Marcel floating into mind.

I shuffled closer to my friend, angling myself so I didn't have to look at him any more than necessary. I didn't know what I was about to offer, I couldn't know, I didn't want to know. I offered anyway, I held out my wrist to him.

"Are you sure?"

"No." I kept my arm steady in front of him.

He waited, giving me a chance to back down. I didn't. I wouldn't. I couldn't.

"This is going to be unpleasant." He grabbed my wrist and lowered it to his mouth. "I'm sorry."

He hesitated, one last chance for me to change my mind, before his lips brushed against my skin and my body exploded inwards. I felt everything all at once. Every emotion, every feeling, sensation, experience, all of it in one single moment, and then another and another, lasting for an eternity packed into a second.

My whole life happened then and there, from birth to death. All I'd experienced so far, all I was yet to experience, and all I would never experience.

All he'd experienced. For a brief moment I became him, I became Lucien and I knew him in a way no one could ever know someone else.

It all vanished and somehow that was worse. I was plain old me again and it was too much. Or maybe too little. It was a different kind of overwhelming and more than my body could handle. I slumped down next to him and closed my eyes.

When I opened them next it was dark out except for a small fire in the corner of the room. He was tending to the flames when I stirred.

"Welcome back. How are you feeling?" He asked, refusing to look away from the fire.

"I've been better. Yourself?"

He turned his body slightly to show me his abdomen, this time all his internal organs were hidden as they were supposed to be, hidden beneath his unblemished skin. There wasn't even a scratch. Other than his ruined shirt and puddles of blood on the floor, there was no sign that he'd been injured. No scar tissue, no dried blood on his body, nothing to indicate he was anything other than fit and healthy.

"I'm fine."

"That's... Yeah, fine." I had many questions somewhere. There was no rush to find them. "Water?"

"Only whatever's left in your canteen. Should be more than enough for you." He replied, passing it towards me. "When you're ready we should start heading back."

"Is it safe?"

"Enough." He paused and softened slightly, intentionally. "It's safe enough. We might have to take the long route back, avoid the roads. I know the way."

I nodded and sipped some water. I offered it to him. His facial expression wasn't subtle and confirmed what I'd already known.

Why would someone like him need water? Did I need water? I took another sip while I contemplated it.

I stood up and secured my canteen to my belt. I met his gaze and then nodded again. He reached out, grabbed the door handle and yanked it open, boards and nails clattering to his feet. It took him a bit of effort, it would have taken me hours with the right tools.

He led the way back. Slow and steady, overly cautious in my opinion. There was a burst of gunfire, some distant shouting, everything far and behind us. I followed his lead, nonetheless. When he walked upright and confident, I did the same. When he crouched low into the undergrowth, I matched his position.

At one point he scaled a tree, nothing said just a hand offered. I didn't take it. I didn't need it. I was right there beside him. I could just about make out the hint of a smile. Approval I assumed. Pride, I hoped.

The tree we were in overlooked the road, it wasn't the closest to the track but it gave us a decent view and some decent cover from anyone who may have passed. It was the road back to camp, the last stretch of our journey. I just wanted to get it over with, but he had other plans.

We balanced there in silence for a while, no obvious reason why we needed to hide in such a way. I'd accepted there was a lot I didn't understand about this war, things I was only just starting to grasp, things he was clearly very familiar with.

So we sat there, and we waited, and we watched as a small group of people walked into view. They were visibly armed, guns held ready for a fight, walking slow and sticking to the grass to muffle their footsteps.

As if on cue, Lucien jumped out of the tree and raced towards them while several other figures around us did the same. The shock of realising we hadn't been alone slowed me down, but not by much.

I got to the group just as the gunfire started. They were aiming wildly, or not even aiming, perhaps, just firing into the darkness around them. They were dropping like flies, they never stood a chance.

I hadn't brought a gun, just a knife. Any other situation and that would have meant death for me. I didn't need a gun. I'm not even sure I needed a knife, I wasn't ready for that realisation though. I grabbed one of them, pushing his gun up and away, slipping my blade into his side.

I realised the gun had been pointing square at Jules, I realised this at about the same time he did and a brief "thanks" echoed in my mind before I got distracted by the task at hand. I took out a couple more people and then the fight was over and I was left facing the night crew. They were watching me as I finished the last guy, and then watched me as I walked over to join them.

"Good job." Emile said, slapping my shoulder in camaraderie. "Lucien did well to find you. You've earnt a place amongst us, if that's something you want. It's your choice."

I didn't hesitate. I didn't think it through at all. I just accepted and that was that. Together, as a group that I was now firmly a part of, we made our way back to base, my limp long since forgotten.

A SINGLE ROSE

Jesse

When I first found out, I was ecstatic. I'd always wanted to change the world, and this was the perfect opportunity. I could freeze time. I could pause whenever I wanted for as long as I wanted. I could even rewind if I tried hard enough. It hurt, but I could do it. I thought I was invincible.

Someone makes a swing for my head? Pause and move out of the way. Someone in the road? Pause and drag them to safety. Someone robbing a store? Pause and incapacitate them. I thought there was no way it could go badly.

I was tentative at first. I'd avoid getting into anything obviously violent, I'd separate what I could without putting myself into danger. I'd take people to the hospital, move them out of the way of what was about to hurt them and get them any immediate help they needed. I'd return lost valuables to the person just mugged.

But I got arrogant. News spread of these mysterious occurrences. I wasn't being discrete, after all. People don't just show up at the doctor's over a mile away from their home without people asking questions.

I loved the attention. It was everywhere, you couldn't walk down the street without hearing about something I'd done. I visited a neighbouring city and even they knew about me.

It wasn't enough. Nobody knew it was me, so it wasn't my attention. It didn't count. I needed recognition. I needed people to know it was me, but I didn't want people knowing it was me. I liked the anonymity.

Instead I started leaving calling cards. A single rose. An elegant way to link everything I'd done. They weren't the easiest to get hold of, they didn't like the local soil, but we had merchants coming through often enough, and I managed to cultivate a fair few at home.

Rumours started spreading, gossip that made me out to be this incredible human, far more impressive than I had ever been considered before. Everyone loved me. The calling card wasn't enough.

I started lingering in places, letting people actually see me. Some even recognised me. I always acted coy when asked, I denied what was being said, but only just. That only helped the rumours. The more I smiled my "no, I'm flattered you think I could I do such a thing," the more people lapped it up.

It became the city's worst kept secret. Everyone knew, but it was fun to play along. Occasionally I was gifted a rose with a wink. I tried to return them when I could, especially the more distinct ones.

I'd never been confident before, I'd never had reason to be. Now, though, I had no reason not to be. I was getting attention for the first time in my life. I was getting noticed. And best of all, I had all the time in the world.

There was still crime going on, I couldn't be everywhere and I missed plenty, but that fuelled the rumours. It was thrilling. I had so much fun playing my role to perfection. I even started taking on bigger hits, a bank robbery, a train heist, I was invincible.

Nobody knew exactly what my powers were, there was plenty of speculation that I refused to confirm or deny. I wasn't a God, I was missing too much, but I couldn't be simply human. No human could pull off the feats I was achieving. Somewhere in between, the best of both. I liked that.

I wasn't just a human. I was more than that. I was finally me. I was finally the person I was destined to be. I got all the glory. I got arrogant.

I never thought to explore much. I did my job, fulfilled my responsibility, and then returned to my correct spot. I'd freeze time, do the bare minimum, and soak up the easy win.

I thought I was the only one. I had no reason to believe I wasn't. How could anybody else have such an incredible power as me? How could anyone else deserve such greatness? I decided they didn't. They couldn't. It was only ever me. I had no reason to think about the outlandish what if's of someone else sharing this power. I had no need to know how it worked, I didn't care to think about that stuff.

Apparently someone else had.

Looking back, all the signs were there. A weird feeling, like time had jumped despite only a second or so having passed. The occasional wave of nausea upon freezing time, sometimes requiring a second attempt to unfreeze. I didn't know those things weren't normal. None of it was normal. Those aspects were all just a part of my new normal. I didn't think to question them.

I ignored it all. Deciding it was the nerves, my general health, or the stress of needing to impress. Performance issues, you know. Stage fright. It was still a stage, even if I was behind the curtain most of the time.

There was an occasion where I thought I saw movement, something off in the distance just on my periphery. I was at my peak, I was strong and nowhere near my limits, I should have investigated but there was a knife near a woman's chest and that took priority. I had a job to do. I had a role to play.

I could have wandered off and came back a week later and that knife wouldn't have moved an inch, it wouldn't have made any progress and yet I couldn't just leave it there. I had to rearrange the scene into something more favourable and by the time that was done, there was no mysterious movement on the horizon.

There was nothing to make me suspicious. It had been a trick of the light, of course, that was all it could have been. Light patterns didn't always react how I'd expected, that was perfectly normal.

I cast the thought aside and restarted time. I felt nauseous. It stuttered but remained frozen.

I tried again. It worked. It started. I felt that weird jump sensation and a knife slip into my back.

Everything clicked into place. All the stuff I'd wilfully ignored, all the stuff I'd accidentally ignored, the person I'd somehow ignored for all those years.

They grabbed my arm and froze time. I wasn't frozen but I was in shock. I was spun to face my assailant. Our eyes locked and I recognised them. A neighbour. I'd thought an admirer.

I wasn't special. Time started and I had no control over it. I was stood in the middle of the street with blood pooling at my feet. I was weak and falling and everything was fading as someone caught me and carried me to the nearest doctor.

My saviour. The same person who'd attacked me. They were now the one being celebrated.

I didn't want to wake up. I wish I hadn't. My body wished I hadn't. The world wished I hadn't.

There was plenty of sympathy on the surface. Plenty of roses I no longer needed. It was all for show. I could see what they were really saying. Their affections had moved elsewhere.

I wasn't of use anymore. I was an inconvenience they were waiting to leave behind. I'd overstayed my welcome. I couldn't go anywhere alone. I couldn't eat. I couldn't sleep. I couldn't function. Worst of all, I'd lost my power.

There was literally no need to keep me around. Once the spotlight had shifted far enough, once they'd ran out of pity, I was abandoned.

Except they were wrong. I hadn't lost my powers. I knew better than to use them liberally. I had to bide my time. I had to play it safe.

I wasn't weak and pathetic. I was traumatised and a long way off healing, physically and otherwise, but that gave me time to plot.

It took some time to get it all figured out. There was no rush. I needed to re-find myself, set my life back on the expected track. Make friends. Others that had been abandoned, perhaps not exactly like I had, but close enough.

It didn't take much to find them, to convince them, to start putting my plans into motion. They just needed that little push in the right direction, that's all it took. One tiny nudge.

The city that once adored me had turned its back on me, so I returned the favour. It was the least I could do, really. I was special again. Everything was exciting again. I was going to burn them all to the ground just like they had done to me.

SPACEWALK

Lilah

There was something almost magical about spacewalks. The chance to experience space, like actual space without the confines of the metal box we lived in. It was something that never got old. Just floating in front of potentially millions of miles of nothingness, of void scattered with the occasional star, or a bit of debris, or whatever else happened to be drifting out there. Just being a tiny little thing on the edge of so much vastness, it has a way of leaving anyone in awe.

I once saw some tough American guy cry on his first day out of the station. He gestured down towards the Earth, it was clear over the states that day. He told us about his wife and child, about how proud they were of him. Someone made a comment about how they were probably looking up, right in that moment, thinking that exact same thing. Instant tears. Never seen the guy laugh, let alone cry.

To be honest until that point I'd pegged him as kind of a douche-bag. Never saying anything more than a few words unless a job absolutely necessitated it. Pretty much ignored any display of emotion from any of the rest of us, occasionally even knowingly saying the least useful thing during tough times. Like, he usually wasn't malicious or cruel, just wilfully clueless when it came to stuff like that. Don't tell him I've said any of this, yeah?

Anyway, seeing a guy like that cry? Kinda softened my opinion of people a bit. It wasn't that he didn't have a caring side, he just didn't show it, like, ever. If it wasn't for that spacewalk, I'd probably still consider him a dickhead. More of a dickhead. He's less of a dickhead than I originally presumed. You can tell him that bit, if you like.

Sorry, got a bit side tracked there.

What was I supposed to be saying?

Right... It was my turn to go out and do some standard stuff, nothing we weren't all familiar with. I hadn't had the opportunity in a while so everyone decided it was only fair.

Everything was going smooth until they tried to bring me back in. Something got jammed and the umbilical wouldn't reel, had to just wait out there while they fixed it.

In a situation like that, there's really not much you can do except relax and enjoy the view. So that's what I did.

Naturally, like anyone else staring out into the abyss, I thought about my own mortality, about higher powers and what else was out there beyond our little world, about what pizza I'd get when I got home. I missed pizza more than I missed home. Mostly I just missed my cat. I wonder if she missed me... She probably did. She was an affectionate little thing, I treated her like a God.

Looking down at it all I almost felt like a God myself, and yet I felt so small, so insignificant. I wonder, if God does exist, maybe he feels the same, looking down at that magnificent planet full of magnificent people doing their own magnificent little things. I couldn't see God, but I could see why others would see him, whether through a conclusion of creation or a fear of the unknown, or even just a desire to not be quite so alone. I'd never been one for religion, still aren't really, but I do understand those that are a little better now than I did.

What I didn't understand, couldn't understand, was the fear they must have felt. I was an outsider to it all, a watcher. I didn't experience what was going on down there, but I saw it. I saw it all. I had a front row seat, after all.

Technically we all expected it, there'd been speculation for months. Denial, jokes, rumours, everyone was talking about it. Who'd be the first to go? Who'd remain? Apparently people were making bets, like actual money bets. I don't know why, it's not like anybody can cash in on that win. Then again, the most I'd ever bet was a month on garbage disposal. Never really got the appeal of gambling and I guess I never will.

Plus, it's not like I can just ask someone, either. Hey corpse, why'd you bet on who'd be the one to kill you? Probably would have to wait a while for that answer. I can live with not knowing. I can live with not knowing a lot of things. I don't know why all this happened, don't even know if I want to know.

I think I want to live not knowing that one.

From where I was, it started with one explosion. Everything was normal and then it wasn't. Saying that, there was a tornado over Japan which was pretty cool to see. I don't remember the last time I heard about one of them. Are they rare? I don't know if they're rare or not. Either way, bad day for those guys.

Britain on the other hand, completely cloudless day. Ok, morning. I can't really speak for the rest of the day, and even without the nukes there was an ominous cloud drifting towards the eastern coast.

Of course, after the nukes there wasn't really much to see. After the first one landed, a few more followed suit, scattering across the globe as retaliation kicked in and allies took revenge. It was probably all automated at that point.

I don't think the initial explosions would have killed everyone. I guess, the radiation might have taken its course and finished the job off proper if there'd have been enough time for it but there just wasn't. So much happened. The weather went completely nuts. And then naturally Yellowstone did its thing, I mean it was apparently kind of overdue, and a bunch of other volcanoes followed suit.

The dust from the bombs and the dust from the eruptions and the storms, everything was just covered. It stopped being the blue planet and became the grey one.

That's a sight I'll never forget. None of us will. No one could survive that. We all knew it, even before you told us. Although, we still had hope. We checked the radios daily, just in case. Sent a signal out almost hourly, almost obsessively. Nothing back, obviously.

We were up there a few weeks, staring down at the grey swirls of the dust storms and mayhem beneath them. Wasn't easy for any of us, lost a couple of the crew during that time. Made things even harder.

Saved on rations for a bit though, so silver linings and whatever. Their sacrifice was our survival, food and oxygen and stuff wouldn't have lasted if they'd stuck around. Maybe they knew. I don't know. I don't want to know.

Things would have gotten bad if you hadn't shown up. Well, worse. We were all on the edge. Hard not to be with supplies running short and the destruction of the world out the window. You saved us. Don't think we can ever repay that.

ROAD TRIP

Mahina

We'd made it about halfway into our road trip. I hadn't arranged anything, just been invited along and took up the opportunity in a heartbeat. Those of us, well, those of them, that could drive, took it in turns to do so. I got to sit pretty in the backseat and enjoy the views.

Someone had found some lovely little cabins for us to spend a couple of days before moving on to wherever the next place was. There were a handful of them, spaced out on the edge of a clearing that backed onto some dense woodland, something to explore the following day. That was the plan.

Someone got chatting to a family in one of the neighbouring cabins, apparently they were just on their way home after a pilgrimage. I didn't find out anything more specific, but they shared the location. They thought it might intrigue us, thought it would be an interesting spot for us to include on our journey. A stone circle, some ancient remnant they'd been visiting regularly for generations. A place of power, they called it.

That got relayed back to the rest of us and set everyone at ease, obviously we'd been called here for a reason and that family had given us the direction we needed. We all went to bed in good humour, eager for the following day.

Except I couldn't sleep. Everyone sounded settled, there was some light snoring though mostly from the man next to me. He was definitely at ease. I was desperate to join him in that. He looked so peaceful and comfortable and I just lay there as my anxiety grew until I couldn't lie there anymore.

I got up to get a drink, give myself something to do, try and get some tension out of my body. Instead, I found Jonas sitting on the porch. He invited me to join him, so I made us both a chamomile tea and pulled up a chair next to him.

Apparently he was also on edge. He couldn't tell me why, much in the same way I couldn't explain my own growing tension. We chatted a little, forced our way through some topics until it wasn't worthwhile. The chamomile wasn't helping.

We settled on silence for bit, neither of us comfortable but not quite ready for bed either. We just watched the stars, beautiful and bright and almost distracting enough to miss the deer that walked into view.

I felt nauseous. I broke the silence. I begged him to go inside, to lock the door, to get away from whatever it was.

A deer. It was just a deer. We'd seen plenty on our travels. It looked exactly the same as all the other ones we'd spotted. He sat there and watched it in the exact same way as all the others, situation obliging.

I couldn't leave him there. Such a deep fear had settled into my bones and I couldn't let him face that alone, especially when he seemingly couldn't feel it.

Except he wasn't moving at all. He'd been rocking slightly in his chair, tapping his fingers on the armrest, but now he was still. He was solid. Frozen. It certainly wasn't a relaxed stillness, but he didn't respond to me, either. He sat and he watched and I begged. That is, until the deer stood up.

It's front hooves slowly lifted from the ground as it's body lifted upwards. I felt it's eyes locked onto me as it settled back onto it's hind legs and screamed.

I felt a hand grasp my arm and drag me inside. I heard the door slam and the lock click. I watched as the deer took a step towards us, then another, and another, before a curtain blocked my view and I was free again.

There was another scream and those same light snores drifting through the cabin.

"Can't they hear it?" I whispered, turning to finally meet the gaze of my friend.

"Hear what?" He asked, fear and confusion written across his face.

Another scream.

"That! Can't you hear that?" He shook his head slowly.

"What can you hear? What's happening?" He asked carefully.

The door knocked. My body whipped towards the sound whilst also trying to get as much distance between me and it. I nearly tripped over the sofa. His hands grasped me firmly, guiding me to a sitting position before crouching down in front of me.

"I don't know what's going on, I don't know what's out there, but that door stays shut, you hear me?" I nodded and it screamed again. "I don't care what you hear out there, you keep it shut."

I swallowed painfully, doing everything I could to push my fear down. "Door stays shut. No matter what."

It screamed and I recognised it and I couldn't leave her out there in danger or hurt or-

I was halfway to the door before I could stop myself. I did stop myself. Jonas had managed to put himself in the way, but it wasn't needed. Not really.

"She's not out there. She's at home. She's safe." I whispered. "Right?"

"Who?"

"My sister. She's safe and she's fine and she's not here, right?"

"She drove you to the airport and she left you there, you remember that? You got on that plane without her. She can't be here."

"She can't be here. But how does it know what she sounds like?"

"I don't know. I don't know what you're hearing. There's some wind maybe, that's it."

"What's happening?" I couldn't hold back any longer, I felt the tears stream down my face and felt him guide me back to the sofa, comfortably away from the door.

He didn't answer me. He didn't know. He just let me cry and watched helplessly every time my body shuddered in response to the noises he couldn't hear.

His gaze drifted behind me, towards my bedroom and the snoring. "Shall I wake up him up?"

I almost said yes. I wanted to. I needed him, I needed the comfort and reassurance but then it was his screams coming from outside and I couldn't say yes. I couldn't drag him into this. Whatever it was, I didn't want him involved. I couldn't do that to him.

I shook my head. I forced myself over to the bedroom and looked at him. He looked calm. He looked safe. He was blissfully unaware and I couldn't wake him from that. I couldn't bring him into my nightmare. I couldn't do that to him.

"He's driving tomorrow. We're leaving this place so that'll be a longer than planned drive, right? So he'll need his rest?"

Another scream.

"We can rearrange. Everyone will understand-"

"Understand what? That I'm hallucinating? That I'm losing my goddamn mind?"

"I saw it too. Whatever that thing is, it's targeting you. That doesn't mean you're crazy."

"No, it means I'm taking the hit so the rest of you don't have to." I don't know where that thought came from, I didn't know how accurate it was, but I believed it and I watched his face as the realisation kicked in for him. He believed it too. "There's no need to drag anyone else into this. I'm taking the hit. I'll take all of it."

A knock, this time from the back wall.

"I don't know how much longer I'll be able to stay awake for."

"I'll take the hit." I reconfirmed. "All of it. Go get some sleep."

A beg for help. My sisters voice. It wasn't her. It couldn't be her.

I didn't want to be alone. I really didn't want to be alone. But there was an isolation I couldn't describe, something about sitting next to someone while having such a profoundly different experience... it felt so alienating. I almost felt more alone with him there. I knew bringing more people into the situation could only make that feeling worse.

"There's nothing you can do for me. Take the key with you. Rest. I can sleep in the car tomorrow while you make sure we all get out of here."

"I messaged the others. Told them to stay inside. I haven't had a response yet. I assume they're all asleep."

A scream. One of the girls from the other cabin,

"Good. It's not her. They're safe. I don't have to worry about them."

"You don't have to worry about them." He paused for a moment, looking for the right words, looking for something useful to say. "None of it is real. Okay? You can hear it and that's real but it's not real."

"It's not real. Door stays shut." I repeated it a few times. Even after he left, I repeated it to myself. It became a little mantra. Every time the voice changed, every time it mimicked someone new, I repeated it to myself.

It's not real. Door stays shut. It's not real. Door stays shut. It's not real. Door stays shut.

At some point threats got thrown into the mix, by my loved one's voices and towards my loved one's. I can't repeat them. I won't. I won't ever tell anyone what got said to me. I can share the easy stuff, that's a small fraction of it all. But soon enough everything picked up in intensity.

At first there were gaps in-between each scream, knock, beg, or threat.

And then it was one after the other.

And then they overlapped.

It became constant, just everything all at once and there was nothing I could do about it. There was nothing I could do about anything. I just sat on the sofa, headphones blasting music as loud as my phone would allow.

I cried. I sobbed, hand over my mouth to muffle the noise as best I could. I didn't want to wake anyone but it didn't take long before I stopped caring about that. I couldn't care. I didn't have anything left in me to care.

It's not real. Door stays shut.

But what if it was real? What if there were people out there? The amount of pain someone would have to be in to make those noises...

It's not real. Door stays shut.

Did the others get the message to stay inside? Their voices were in the mix, they could have heard our voices, they could have gone out to investigate, they could have been real cries for help. The desperate knocking on the door could have been them, like actually them, the real them.

It's not real. Door stays shut.

Or the family next door. They had a little girl. If she saw a deer, would she run out to see it? Would she fall for whatever trick it was playing? Was she out there, hurt and afraid? Or worse?

It's not real. Door stays shut.

Let us in! Please! It's not safe out here! Why are you doing this to us? Why won't you help us? How could you leave us out here? We need your help! Help us! Please! You have to help us!

Please.

That last bit was a whisper. No more overlap, no more noise, just a single please, whispered right into my ear, and that was it. I cautiously shifted my headphones and was met with such a glorious silence, broken only by the music that was still playing and that light snoring from the other room.

It was over. I was so tired. I could sleep, finally. The sun was just coming up but I could sleep. I had to. I had nothing left.

I don't know how long I was asleep for. Everyone else had gotten up, started and finished packing, and were just waiting on me. I sat up, not quite ready to face the day, but within a couple of minutes I was handed a drink, some food, and a gentle kiss on the forehead. I flinched, I just wasn't ready. He left me to it, they all did.

I couldn't figure out what tension was in the air, concern maybe? Guilt? I was too tired to guess, too tired to ask. Nobody asked me anything. I assume they'd had it all explained already, all of what could be explained, at least.

They gently bundled me into the car, shielding me from the woodland, and we left. It was over. I watched the cabins disappear behind us and slowly allowed my body to drift off again. It was over and we were safe.

Eventually I felt the car come to a stop, I figured we must have arrived at wherever we were going, I wasn't the one planning so I didn't need to know details like that. Everything felt fuzzy so I was glad to be somewhere with an actual bed. I was lucky to be able to sleep in the car, but obviously it didn't compare to an actual bed.

I said that out loud. I'm pretty sure I did. Nobody acknowledged it. They were all chatting and laughing and setting themselves up for the night ahead. Someone had found some lovely little cabins, spaced out on the edge of a clearing. A plan was soon made up to explore the surrounding woodland the following day.

Except I didn't want to. The idea terrified me. Perhaps I could just spend the day at the cabin, I was exhausted for some reason, I knew a day of rest would do me some good.

I said that out loud. I'm pretty sure I did. Nobody acknowledged it. Nobody acknowledged anything I said. There were times a response looked like it was aimed at me, but it didn't quite fit with what I'd said.

Someone got chatting to one of the neighbouring cabins, a family heading home from a pilgrimage apparently. Their little girl was playing in the clearing, she must have found something and screamed in... delight? She looked excited? She looked pleased with herself, holding her haul high in the air and racing over to her parents to show it off.

Delight. It must have been delight.

But something was wrong. I felt so nauseous. I was exhausted. I couldn't do it again.

I couldn't do what again? We'd only just arrived?

There were a few chairs strewn across the porch, I gathered them up into something a little more sociable and sat down, beckoning my boyfriend over. He laughed and said something about making myself at home before leaning over and kissing the air above the chair next to me.

I was sat in the wrong chair. I wasn't following the script. I'd gone wrong somewhere. We'd been there before. I was so close to remembering.

That girl's scream. Delight. It had to be delight. It couldn't be anything else.

Terror. That's what I'd heard. Except it wasn't from her. It was from last time. It was from...

The deer.

I remembered. All of it. I threw up. But I remembered. And nobody was acknowledging me. They sat around the table eating food. I watched as the bowl I was supposed to have slowly emptied, just like everyone else's, but I wasn't there. I was breaking the script. I wasn't playing their game. I couldn't do it again. There was nothing I could do.

I pleaded with everyone. I grabbed whoever was close and did everything I could to drag them out of there. I wasn't strong enough. Nobody was. I was out of time, out of place. I had no hope of pulling anyone off of their track.

I moved furniture and they just sat in the original spot anyway. I threw someone's drink and they went through the normal motions regardless. I even slapped someone, full force, and I just bounced off them. They didn't flinch, didn't react, didn't feel a thing.

I grabbed a knife and... put it right back down again. I couldn't do that. I'd long since realised I couldn't change anything, but that wasn't a risk I was willing to take. I didn't know the rules. I didn't understand what I'd got myself into.

Everyone went to bed and I knew I was running out of time.

I couldn't face going out there. I didn't need to. Everything was playing out in the same way anyway, I didn't need to follow the script, the outcome was inevitable.

I thought about going out there, meeting it in that clearing before it had a chance to start. My body wouldn't oblige. It froze up. I couldn't move. The dread I felt at that idea was debilitating.

I briefly considered locking Jonas outside. I wondered if that would break the loop, sacrifice him. The guilt though, I couldn't do that either. I knew that even before I considered it. I'd already refused to abandon him out there. This time wasn't going to be any different.

There was a scream and it didn't matter anymore. He was inside and the door firmly closed. The deer was stood out there, looking at me. I was in the wrong place, I knew I was in the wrong place, and yet it looked at me anyway. It was breaking the script as well. Did that mean it remembered as well

Yes.

That same whispered voice, right into my ear.

Jonas was sat on the sofa, comforting a person who wasn't there. I watched him, followed him as he left 'me' there. He didn't go to bed immediately, he sat on the edge and stared off into space for a few moments.

He looked up, looked right at me.

"Are you there?" He asked quietly.

I didn't know that he was talking to me, the eye contact was just slightly off, but it was close enough to be disconcerting. I had to respond. "Yes."

"I'm not here, not like you are. I don't have long. It's too late to change it." He chose his words carefully.

"I know." I didn't know changing it had been an option at all. "Why me?"

"You looked at it."

"So did you?"

He didn't respond to that.

"I'm sorry."

He looked away and that was it. Something had shifted. Jonas was back on his rails, though substantially paler than he had been only moments before. I left him to it, closing the door behind me.

Suddenly I had several tortuous hours to kill. I wasn't prepared to fall into that same sobbing hole, not when there was a whole range of other emotions to feel. This time I had access to anger and so much more, the power of hindsight. Foresight? I knew what I was in for and I refused to play my role.

I was also pretty confident my actions wouldn't have lasting consequences. So, what would it matter if I smashed up the place?

At some point I got it into my head that if I could leave, if I could get to the car then I'd be able to break out of the loop. Legally I couldn't drive, but I knew enough to figure it out.

The knocking was coming from the other side of the cabin when I first tried the door, if I was going to do something stupid then I had to be smart about it.

The lock clicked open and the door remained solidly in its frame. I pulled at it with all my weight. I decided that I just forgot which way it swung so I tried pushing. I threw myself at it. Over and over.

A new tactic was needed. I shifted my attention to the window and grabbed a chair. I stopped paying attention to where the noises were coming from. I didn't care. I needed to get out. I couldn't do it again.

The chair shattered. The glass stayed perfectly intact. Not even a scratch. I tried again and again until I ran out of chairs. I figured the sofa was a little too unwieldy for me to lift.

Nobody's luggage was heavy enough to bother with. A soft backpack wouldn't do anything a chair couldn't. A baseball bat perhaps? I knew the group had one, I didn't know it had been left with us until I stumbled upon it.

I swung at the window over and over and over until I could barely lift it anymore. I wasted some time and not much else. I definitely wasn't the strongest amongst us, but I had some muscle to me, enough that I should have fractured the glass, at the very least marked it in some way, dented the wood on the occasions I missed the window. Nothing I did made any difference.

I only stopped because my arms were failing me. The noise was constant by that point. It was everywhere. I couldn't break my way out. But there were other ways to leave.

I grabbed the knife again. My actions had no real affect, so what would happen? Would it work? Could it?

I should have started small but I was desperate. I needed out. I put the tip to my throat and pushed it through.

The pain was unimaginable. Indescribable. As was the relief. It worked. It must have done. I could feel it. I was so tired and in so much pain and not a single drop of blood left my body.

I pulled it out and put my fingers to where the hole should have been. My neck was perfectly intact. It hurt so much and yet it didn't do anything. My body was fine.

I watched the knife slip into my abdomen and watched it slip back out again, no damage done. I tried a few more times, a few more places. It was a distraction. That was it. Something I could focus on that wasn't the horrendous noise that was surrounding me.

It was morning once again before I knew. I'd given up on escape. Given up on everything, and just settled onto the floor, back to the door. Knife idly in hand but not doing anything with it. I tuned out as much as I could until I heard that final *please.*

It was over. Once again it was over.

I watched one of the girls open her door and spot 'me' on the sofa. She tiptoed over and gently draped a blanket across 'my' body. She didn't know anything about what happened. It was such a simple act of kindness.

The others soon followed with various looks of confusion and concern aimed at the sofa. They all ended up gathered in the kitchen, someone phoned the other cabin, and Jonas talked them through what happened that first night. It was hard to watch. They all looked horrified.

It was unanimously decided that we would leave. Instant action. We hadn't made much mess, so it went smoothly until Jonas opened the door.

A deer head had been left, pride of place on the porch, upright and facing where I had been on the sofa. He followed its gaze and came to the same conclusion.

I couldn't look away from it. It was left for me. I was vaguely aware of a conversation going on behind me but I didn't care. It was a gift for me.

"Does anyone have gloves?"

"I do. I'll deal with it."

"Put it back into the woods. Don't let her see it."

A pair of blue latex hands reached down and a body blocked my view. He walked off with it as instructed. Someone tipped some water over the blood stain. Everyone avoided it when they carried the luggage out to the car.

The blanket on the sofa stirred slightly and I watched my boyfriend get up and make me breakfast. I couldn't look at his face. I'd avoided it completely. I don't know what he must have felt. I don't want to know.

It was nearly time to leave. I didn't know what to do. I didn't know what would happen. My body hurt and I didn't know what that would mean for me when I tried to leave. All I could do was get in the car and slowly drift off as the pain faded and my body relaxed. It was over and I was fine.

I woke up a little while later. Everyone seemed a little off, a little anxious. That was to be expected, surely. We pulled up to our cabins, engine turned off, and everyone stayed put.

"I can't do this again." I mumbled out as soon as I recognised the place.

"We can leave, find somewhere else." The driver made moves to start up the car. It spluttered a few times, it made an effort to start, but couldn't quite manage it. "We'll see if the others can give us a jump. There's leads in the back."

People finally moved. I stayed put. As did Jonas.

"I don't know if you're going to have a choice." He finally said.

"There's always a choice. I choose not to. It's not too late this time. I remember. I remember it all. I won't do it again. I can't do it again. Please don't make me do it again." I was sobbing by the end of the sentence. "I choose not to."

The other car pulled up beside us and promptly died. I didn't know anything about cars, so I went inside and shut myself in the bedroom. I could hear them outside, trying to get either of them working. It was a pointless endeavour.

The afternoon passed without incident. On occasion someone would come in to check on me, but I refused to acknowledge them. I was handed food and I put it down without trying any.

The evening kicked in and then bedtime was due, only none of them obliged. I could hear tense chatter coming from the other room, but no sounds of movement.

The chatter stopped suddenly. It was time. I knew that was what that meant, but I didn't hear it. My choice mattered. I chose not to go through it again, so I wasn't.

As if on cue, I heard Jonas speak up. "It's not real. Door stays shut."

"But what if she's out there? I can't leave her!" One of the girls cried.

My choice mattered and it dawned on me what that meant. I'd made my choice because I had the choice. They hadn't had that opportunity.

I couldn't just sit there. I got up and made my way through to the others. All eyes on me as I walked towards them. Nobody spoke up but I saw the telltale flinches. I headed to the window and pushed the curtain back, the bare minimum for only me to see out.

It was stood there, waiting for me.

It was me because it was always going to be me. It was inevitable. I knew how it felt and I couldn't make them go through it.

I was always going to make that choice.

LIGHTHOUSE

Daniil

We'd heard stories. There's always stories. But that's all they are, until you're the one telling it. We were all accustomed to the normal ones, the mermaids, the kraken, the ghost ships. Those stories had been around as long as people had, or close enough, at least.

These ones were new. Or maybe, surviving was new. You need survivors to tell stories. Many ships go missing without a trace, no clues as to what happened. So, maybe these monsters weren't new, maybe ships started to get built sturdier, maybe navigation got more reliable, and maybe we just started getting luckier.

I remember the first time I heard about it. Just some lone drunkard accosting anyone who would listen. He'd lost everyone, that much was obvious. One look at the poor sod gave that away.

Kai was his name, and it was an obvious case of survivors guilt, just making up nonsense to cope with the loss. He was the navigator, it was his fault the ship ran aground. Not that he admitted that. No one would admit to that.

"The lighthouse wasn't supposed to be there!" He would exclaim. "The lighthouse pulled us onto the rocks!"

Frankly that was just an admission of guilt. Lighthouses were surrounded by rocks, that was the point of the off coast ones, to tell you where you were and where the rocks were. He was a seasoned pro, he knew that as well as the rest of us. It was his job to know that.

Who would believe someone like that? I certainly didn't, none of my crew did, and the way everyone else looked at him suggested they didn't either. It was looks of pity, looks of annoyance, looks of curiosity one would regard a bard with an interesting story. Never looks of belief.

We'd just got back from a good haul so I offered him a room, told him to sleep it off, told him I could get him a job in the morning once he'd sobered up. He looked so defeated, so weary and lost and misunderstood. He looked like a kid who just wanted someone to take him seriously.

But he did accept, both offers, and I stuck to my word. Come morning that man had a job. Not as navigator, of course, that would have been foolish of me after everything he'd said. He became a regular deckhand, hard work and minimal responsibility, just what he needed to keep his mind off things.

It was the best decision I could have made. I had no way of knowing that at the time and my second in command was adamant I was making a mistake, I even agreed at the time. I was a man of my word, though, even the drunken ones, and at no point did he make me regret it.

Obviously part of the deal was for him to shut up. I couldn't allow talks of imminent doom on my ship, that was a sure fire way to lose a crew. He negotiated a caveat, one I allowed because of how absurd it sounded.

If he caught wind of the same nonsense that sunk his ship, he could warn us as much as he liked. It was fair game if he genuinely thought we were in danger. Instincts were important, and I had no desire to squash his.

I think at the time I just wanted to give him a chance to redeem himself. He looked painfully similar to my kid, back when we used to sail together. We all had our stories, I knew what it was like to be a survivor, to carry that guilt. Maybe that swayed my views somewhat.

Obviously there was no way he would need to warn us,

though. That was a ridiculous thought that I wouldn't entertain. And yet it weighed on me. I didn't believe him in the slightest, but something had happened. The longer he worked with us the clearer it became, his navigation skills weren't the issue. He was by far better than the guy I'd chosen to fill that role.

Don't get me wrong, my navigator was perfectly adequate but I feared his was losing his sight somewhat. I caught Kai muttering under his breath more than enough times to steer us correctly. He always mysteriously seemed to be in the perfect spot to do so, when needed.

I offered him the job once my navigator retired, once I'd almost forgotten about the original lighthouse nonsense. I wasn't surprised when he declined, disappointed but not surprised. He'd been on my crew for a couple years by that point, he'd more than proved himself and we'd not encountered any mysterious lighthouses.

Of course we'd found plenty other mysteries, as was the way with the open ocean. Ghost ships, siren songs, giant tentacles thankfully far off in the distance. We weren't strangers to the supernatural, not by any means. But it was all well-known stuff, none of the new nonsense he'd been spouting when we'd first met.

We all knew how it worked, except for a couple of the younger lads, but they were good and followed our lead with only minor prompting. We did lose one to the siren song, I will admit. He was stubborn and strong and the allure was too great for him.

He jumped, without a second thought. Someone made a grab for him but was that little bit too slow. He dipped below the waves and that was it. If he'd have surfaced we would have sent someone down there to fetch him. As it was... I wasn't willing to risk any more of my crew for a lost cause. That was my burden to carry, as was all the others.

Once we were out of their territory we held a memorial. Something small. We hadn't known him long and we didn't have the resources for much else. It was for the younger lads more than anything else. I know it shook them up. Everyone's first is always rough. I'm pretty sure I threw up after mine.

Us older ones had been out there so long we thought we'd seen it all. We had seen it all, and multiple times at that. We were seasoned pros. Lighthouses should have been safe. In fact, we'd passed multiple of them, all exactly where they were supposed to be and all perfectly benign. They were functional and helpful, as they were made to be.

I started having my doubts when I noticed an unexpected light on the horizon. This was no green flash, or other such phenomena, it did just look like a lighthouse through low clouds. Most of my men were below deck, sleeping the dreary weather away while they could. The rest of us gathered on the deck to observe it.

My navigator was the one who pointed it out. He apologised for getting us lost, said he had no idea where we were because the route he'd charted didn't take us anywhere near any known lighthouses.

I sent someone to fetch Kai, discretely. We were slow moving and it was seemingly far off so I didn't worry about halting us, that could wait until it was necessary. I did tell everyone to be ready, if we needed to wake up the rest and jump into action then I needed those present to be prepared.

The lighting on my boat was poor but even so I noticed Kai visibly pale when he was arrived and noticed what we were all staring at.

"What do you think?" I asked him.

"May I speak freely?"

"That is why I called you up here."

"Fuck this."

I shared his sentiments. "You've been keeping track of our location, correct?"

"Of course."

"Could we have steered off course enough for this to be expected?"

"Not without a typhoon."

"You're that confident?"

"Of course."

"Wake the crew. Turn us around."

"Uh, Captain?" One of the youngsters spoke up. "Captain, they changed their direction, and their flag?"

We'd all been busy watching the light, we hadn't noticed what was going on around us and he was right. Another ship was rapidly approaching, flying the bloody red flag.

"Wake the crew up." I yelled. Everyone had got stuck in paralysis, they needed the extra prompt into motion.

We couldn't go back and we couldn't go forward. We didn't have time to turn either, they'd have caught up too easily. We were a cargo vessel, we weren't kitted out for much of a fight, especially not against a no mercy crew. All we could hope for was to outrun them.

"Kai, what do you remember about that lighthouse thing? How close can we pass it by?"

"How should I know?"

"Figure it out!" I know I gave him an impossible task, but we were faced with an impossible situation and no one had the experience he did. "Your job is to strategise, I don't want you doing anything else. We have an advantage they don't and we have to utilise that. Remember everything you can."

"What are you planning?"

"If they think that's a normal lighthouse then they're probably planning on running us aground. Chase us into the shallows, sink us, salvage whatever they can from the shallower water." I talked while I pulled ropes. "Find us the advantage."

"And if there isn't one?"

I paused and looked at him, properly looked at him. You could never really know when a goodbye was on the horizon, but it sure did look like ours was approaching. "Then it was nice knowing you."

It was a stupid idea. Genuinely foolish. But they had the better vessel and a dumbass plan was the best I had. It was literally better than nothing. That was it. Bait them into destruction and use the distraction to high-tail out of there.

We picked up speed as best we could and I gave the order to change course, aim directly for the lighthouse. They were likely going to try and pin us between them and the structure, between them and the rocks. I didn't want them on our outside, I couldn't have them knowing which way we were going. That was an advantage I had to utilise until I had a better one.

Kai wasn't subtle about his thoughts, any other occasions and he'd have been kicked off my ship for such a thing. As it was, everything he said was accurate. I talked him through my logic, it felt more like talking myself through it.

It didn't look like he was listening. It looked like he was cursing the day we met before storming off, occupying himself with some meaningless busy work.

He reappeared beside me a few minutes later.

"Douse the lamps."

I sent out the order, no questions asked. Not until it had been done, at least.

"Why?"

"We're far enough ahead of them our lights are going to give away our direction."

He was right, but it wasn't enough. There was something he wasn't telling me. The moon was shining off our sails, we couldn't remove them without losing the speed and that was as good as surrender. We were far too easy to track, our lamps didn't make that much difference.

I didn't say anything. I watched him. He met my gaze, shuffled awkwardly, and looked away. I didn't need to say anything.

"I might be wrong."

"You can't make the situation any worse."

He paused, considered whatever it was he needed to consider, and then spoke up. "Bare bones crew, as few people visible as possible."

I sent out the order. The youngsters were the first to be sent down. Stay ready. Stay out of sight. The rest was on a volunteer basis. Kai talked us through what he thought was needed. Those who were confident they could manage it, they stayed up top. Bare bones crew.

We were running out of time. Either it would work, or it wouldn't. The pirates were nearly upon us and we were nearly within the reach of the light. It was decision time. Left or right.

Left.

They followed suit with ease.

Lower the sails.

They weren't a ramming vessel, the collision would have hurt them as much as us. We had momentum so we didn't come to a halt, but we weren't catching the wind and that made a lot of difference. They caught up fast. Not fast enough.

"Predators like movement. It's a hunt, a fresh kill." Kai finally said. It was a long shot, based on assumptions of assumptions.

"Stay in the shadows! Keep hold and don't move! Whatever happens, don't fucking move!"

The light from the lighthouse, it had been doing its thing, perfectly normal lighthouse light. Until we got close enough, until it's sweep covered over us and it stopped. It lit up my deck and the surrounding water and my ship lurched towards it.

All our momentum was halted. Our forward direction stopped suddenly, in its place a bizarre diagonal. The other ship passed us by, they'd have skimmed our hull if we hadn't have been moved.

They were faster than us, they were far more interesting than us. Kai had been right. My men did as they were told. My men deserved a raise. Kai deserved a raise. The pull from the light stopped.

We stayed in its radius for an agonising amount of time, stuck perfectly still in its gaze. The pirates swung around to face us, to pull up beside us and ready to board. We were fish in a barrel as far as they were concerned.

The light swung over to them before they could reach us and I could breathe again. We watched them lurch in that same horrible diagonal, against the laws of the ocean, against the pull of the tide or the push of the wind, neither of those things affected them anymore.

We watched the crew scramble, try and turn the ship, try and find the wind, try and do anything. Several of them fired off their ropes and I did nothing to intervene, I just watched. A few of them even landed and it didn't matter. All they could do was watch their ship get pulled further and further away, their escape got further and further away.

We all watched as their hull crashed apart, as the water opened up and pulled them in. We heard their screams as they went down with their ship and the light sunk down with them. Suddenly we were all alone in the open ocean.

Nobody moved. We sat there for the rest of the night, probably only a couple of hours but it stretched on and on endlessly until the sun peaked its way over the horizon. We were free.

The ocean was empty, there was no looming structuring, no arcing light, no sign of rocks or land of any sort. If it wasn't for the mess of planks floating around us, there'd have been no sign that anything had gone on.

We stayed put until the sun had fully appeared. I wanted full sight. I wanted to see if there were any survivors in the water. I wanted to give them as much chance as I possibly could. I spotted the sharks before I spotted any people. I didn't keep looking after that. It was time to get going, raise the sail and leave it all behind.

Three of the pirates had made it onto my ship. They hadn't caused any trouble, they'd stood on my deck and witnessed their crew's final moments. They didn't have any fight left in them, not by the time I approached them.

In exchange of their weapons, I offered them safe passage to the nearest harbour. Nobody in their right mind would have said no to that, not after what we'd all been through. They joined us without question, they took up duties and kept to themselves throughout the remainder of the journey.

Everyone was unusually quiet. I couldn't blame them. We had been on a deadline but that came and went and I did nothing to speed us up. I wasn't going to push my men any more than I had to and we were all on edge, I had no desire for any of them to break. Getting them to shore was my priority, cargo be damned.

"How did you survive the first time?" I asked Kai during a quiet moment. "I never believed you before so I didn't need to ask. I'm sorry for that."

"One of the lifeboats fell while we were being pulled in. At some point I got thrown from the ship and found the lifeboat. Got picked up the next day."

"Luck."

"Luck."

"You're a braver man than I am. Thank you." I had nothing else to say on the matter. I had no desire to talk about it ever again and I assumed he felt similarly, I assumed they all did.

When we got to shore, I sold my wares and gave them all what I owed. I sold my ship and shared that out as equally as I could and that was it. That was my last voyage.

AN HEIRLOOM

Theodore

I didn't know that's what it did. I just thought it was a normal camera. It looked like a normal camera and it certainly acted like a normal camera. How was I supposed to know? It was given to me as a normal camera.

My father, as soon as he heard I was interested in taking up photography full-time, he wrapped it up nice and neat and handed it to me on my following birthday. He told me it was special, an heirloom, and I had to be careful with it. It certainly was old, he didn't tell me specifics, just that it had been in the family since its invention. I believed him.

It was mine to carry now, that's what he told me, my responsibility to bear.

It felt good to use, to hold and set up plus it used dry plates which were far more convenient than the available alternatives. I found more freedom in it, which is why that camera felt like a godsend. It helped me kick my business up a notch.

Once I got a good feel for it, I offered is as part of my services professionally. I already was doing that with my old camera, but it was cheap in comparison, and had its limitations. The quality of the pictures I got out of this one were so much better. I honestly couldn't believe it, and the fact that he'd had it the whole time? And this was the first time he'd thought to mention it?

When I thought about it, it felt like a betrayal, all the opportunities we'd missed as a family because he'd hidden this incredible contraption away from us all. Even just selling it, it must have been worth a fortune. Genuinely. It was the best camera

I ever had the privilege to use.

I am glad he didn't sell it. It would have been nice if our family had been set up a little better, but the opportunity I found myself in was worth all those struggles. Plus, I could make that same fortune and then some, so I knew it had all worked out for the best.

I just wanted to look after my family. I wanted to set up a nice little business to make a nice bit of money to get a nice cosy cottage for my wife and then we could be a nice little family. That was all I wanted.

It's not my fault the camera was special. I didn't know, I couldn't know, and then it was too late. You have to understand me, surely? And obviously, it was outlandish, nobody would believe such a thing. It took some time to realise, to get over the disbelief, to actually accept what was happening.

The damage was done by that point. I was booked up so far in advance and I couldn't cancel them. I couldn't turn away the society's elites without risking my own elite status, without putting my family's well-being at risk. It wasn't worth it. It was scary to even think about.

So I didn't think about it. I didn't think about any of it, not really. It got overwhelming very quickly. So I didn't. It wasn't my problem. They were all coming to me freely, after all. They'd have thought I was crazy if I'd tried to tell them the truth. I couldn't do that to my family.

I did consider taking the pictures, taking my payment, and then staging a fire, or some other disaster to destroy the plates. I honestly didn't know if that would help or not. It certainly seemed like the issues only started once I developed them.

I'd already had a well-established business by the time I realised. A lot of one-off celebration type clients. It wasn't until my first repeat. The first time I saw her hollow gaze, gaunt and pale face, slow zombie like movements. Obviously that wasn't enough to convince me, she was just ill and it happened to coincide with our arrangement.

And then I had my second repeat. And my third. The fourth, then the fifth. All the same. That's when I started checking in with previous clients. I offered them a deal, a cheaper service for their loved ones, or whatever was appropriate to their situations.

Everyone was the same. Everyone who had been in the camera had that same mystery illness. The people who'd been around, watching or going about their business in the surrounding area, they were all fine. It was only those who were directly in frame. Even the background apparently. One of the gardeners none of us had paid much attention to had been passing by, even he had been affected.

Obviously none of it made any sense. I didn't know how illnesses worked but these were people I'd shaken hands with, I'd helped pose in some cases, I'd taken money from. If they were getting ill, then why wasn't I? Why was the wife I hadn't touched affected but the husband I'd greeted and interacted with was perfectly fine?

It had something to do with me, that was the only dot I could connect for a while. I knew other photographers who weren't having this problem, as far as I could tell. I poached some clients from a rival, they were fine up until they met me. That was what sealed the idea it was connected to me.

At about the same time, that same photographer was mocking some of the more 'outlandish' beliefs about photography. Travel was a large part of the work, he met a lot of incredible people with a lot of interesting beliefs.

Apparently that included something along the lines of how photos steal people's souls. Of course I laughed along with everyone else, but the idea stuck with me. I couldn't shift it no matter how hard I tried. I spent the next few days thinking through the logistics, mostly about how ridiculous it was.

I ran an experiment. I started with some of the older clients, the ones less likely to notice quality, and then I took on some cheaper clients alongside them, and I used my old camera. I noticed the dip in quality, it was ever so obvious to me, but none of them mentioned it and none of them got the mystery illness.

Clearly it wasn't all cameras that stole people's souls.

Not that that's what mine was doing, I'll never really know exactly what it was. It was all just a bizarre and unfortunate coincidence. None of them died so it wasn't like I was condemning them all to death or anything dreadful like that.

Plus, illness wasn't exactly uncommon. I'm sure a trip to the seaside or other such remedy would have sufficed. That was prescribed to my wife when she was struggling a bit, nowhere near to the same extent but there was an overlap of symptoms.

Perhaps they were all just being a bit dramatic. Or not trying hard enough to get better, not listening to the doctor and whatnot. None of that was my fault.

Honestly, there was nothing I could do.

My wife wanted a nice family portrait. She'd been hinting for years but finally just asked. Obviously I got out my old camera. That wasn't good enough, though. She'd heard me rave on and on about how much better the new one was, she couldn't understand why I'd suddenly opt not to use it.

I couldn't tell her, what would she think of me? She'd think I'd lost my mind. Perhaps I had. A soul stealer, what an absurd thing to believe. That's why I didn't, not really. Not until it came to taking a picture of my wife. It was all just a coincidence but I couldn't do that to her. I couldn't do that to the kids.

So I set up a date. I was a busy man so I had plenty of excuses, it wasn't unreasonable for me to be all booked up for a while but I could set aside a date just for her. Because I loved her. I would do it for her.

Everything was going to plan, she grew increasingly excited

as I grew increasingly rich. I took on extra clients, got us enough money so we wouldn't have to worry for a while. I was setting us up nicely and then my father visited.

He ruined everything. I had it all scheduled. A day later and I would have pulled it off without a hitch.

He was also a photographer, my wife reasoned, he could take the photo so I could be there next to her. What sort of husband would say no to that? A braver one, perhaps.

I was never a brave man.

I got swept up in the moment, I insisted she wait, insisted for our scheduled date. I had no good reason to offer her, so she had no good reason to oblige. This was the opportunity she'd been waiting for. A family portrait, that's all she wanted. I couldn't say no. I stood there next to her. A coward. I couldn't admit to my sins, not even for her.

And then I caught his eye. He knew. He was just as much of a coward as I was. He was worse. He gave me that camera and he knew. He set up my doom, my family's downfall, my business's demise. He took that picture and he knew.

The camera flashed and my mother's illness suddenly made a whole lot more sense. I'd received a picture as a boy, whilst I was off at boarding school and my mother wanted to gift me something nice. Women and their sentiments.

I didn't need to process them. I felt fine, my wife looked fine, so that part of my plan could still go ahead. I didn't know if it would work, I didn't intend to risk her in that way, but it was too late, it was the only option I had left.

The exact day didn't matter anymore, I wasn't on that same deadline, and a part of me was curious. Could I hold her insistence at bay? Could I get the best of both worlds? She had her picture taken like asked and I could stave off the mystery illness by not processing them.

Eventually she forced my hand. I'd processed the portraits of everyone else, I had to collect the money. She reasoned it was her turn to receive her gift. If she hadn't have pushed so much this never would have happened. If she had just accepted my refusal, we would have been fine, we'd have had our happily ever after.

I processed my pictures in a little shed in the garden, I'd often resented it's distance from the house but for once I found myself grateful. As I poured out the gasoline, I was glad it wasn't in the house.

I covered as much as I could, there were a few portraits I hadn't returned yet, I had to make it believable as an accident. I couldn't empty the place first, that would have been far too suspicious. There were portraits and dry plates, even some wet plates from my other cameras. Sat in the centre of it all was that cursed camera, the prized heirloom that had ruined my life. I made sure to douse it.

I stood in that doorway in the middle of the night. As far as anyone knew, I was tucked up in bed. Plausible deniability. It was dark enough, no one would see me out of the window.

I knew it wasn't too late, I could have turned and gone back into the house and taken my chances with my wife. It could have been a perfectly normal camera and I was delusional, connecting a bunch of coincidences and making them about me.

I couldn't risk it. I lit that match and I threw it as close to that awful camera as I could manage and I ran. I tucked myself into bed and my wife was none the wiser. I closed my eyes and I prayed for the fire to do its work.

It wasn't long before there was a pounding on the door. My wife roused before I did, she answered it and then raced back to me, grabbing my shoulders and shaking until I acknowledged her. She was sobbing. Scared and confused and cast in an orange glow.

A neighbour had noticed the fire and sent for help, his wife had ran over to wake us, to get us out of the house just in case. We grabbed what we could, she got the kids, I got the money and we went out into the street for all to see. We were going to be the talk of the town for weeks.

Thankfully the house was fine. The wind was blowing away from it, we got lucky. I hadn't even thought to factor in such a thing. We stayed with the neighbour's until the flames died out, and then a little longer just to be sure.

I dreaded going back out there, dreaded what I'd find when I looked in our garden, in our ashes of a shed. It had been my passion, my life's work, and I'd burnt it to the ground.

Once we were given the all clear, my wife wrapped her arm around mine and gently lead me over there. She knew how much it meant to me and wouldn't make me do it alone. I think that was worse.

It was all ash, it had completely burnt down to the ground, there was nothing left. Nothing except that damned camera, sat exactly where I'd left it, completely untouched.

It was a miracle, my wife insisted.

THEN THERE WAS LIGHT

Thom

There was a click. Then another. And another. A moment passed. Then there was light.

It wasn't much, enough to see the rest of the room without strain, but that was barely anything compared to what we were used to. There was always light, always stars and screens and buttons, and that was all extra on top of the regular 'day' lighting. The window shielding had activated when the lights cut, so even the stars were gone.

"What happened?"

It was a simple question and the silence that followed spoke volumes. There was no response because there was no answer. Everything had been fine, everything had been normal, and then everything went dark.

"Do we know anything?"

A pause. Everyone prodded at their stations, trying to find something of use.

"We lost everything. The systems that were designed to have fail safe after fail safe, all failed. The engines..." A soft voice spoke up but then simmered out. After a deep breath, she carried on. "There's a transmission on the radios, it's hard to understand but, I think they're saying the backup power had to be restored manually. It should have kicked in immediately, some places still haven't... The oxygen levels... They don't know why, they haven't found a cause, not yet at least."

"Tell them we received-"

"I can't. I'm sorry for interrupting, Captain, but I can't. Everything's scrambled, I can't get it to transmit. The frequencies, they just keep changing, they're not supposed to do that. This is old school tech, I was taught everything about it, but not this."

"Figure it out. Until we find out otherwise, we'll treat this like a worst case scenario. We trained for this. We're a team, if you can't fulfil your role then-"

A scream interrupted him, extending for an uncomfortable amount of time, before ceasing. The sudden silence was almost as painful.

The Captain turned to face me and I knew what he was about to say. "Take Avery. Be back in 30. Check that we're safe. Now, everyone, get back to work."

It filled me with dread but I knew I couldn't hesitate, I knew it wasn't worth it, so I walked out the door and didn't look back. I didn't want them to see my face, I could only hold my expression for so long before my real feelings would become apparent.

The door slid closed behind me. Avery must have hesitated, she had been right beside me before I moved. It shouldn't have taken her so long, though I relished the moment to myself. A chance to feel and then compose.

I waited. Maybe the Captain had more to say, maybe something had come up and she would relay the details. I couldn't wait any longer and opened the door myself, and there she was, appearing before me as if no time had passed.

"Oh good, the power's back." She said, explicitly ignoring my attempt to stumble out of her way. The door closed again and the light flickered.

"Let's hope it lasts." I muttered, leading the way down the hall.

"Should we split up? Cover more ground? We don't have long."

She sounded uncertain so I made the decision.

"No, that scream sounded close. Whoever, whatever, caused it shouldn't be too far off. We're safer together."

"Start on the left?"

"Start on the left."

We scanned over every room along that hallway, each of them devoid of any sign of life. Neither of us spoke until we reached the first junction.

"There should be people. Shift change is soon, the next crew should be here for that."

"Something happened," I replied cautiously, "maybe it forced everyone further into the ship."

"We would've heard something."

"We did-"

"Something more. Running, Shouting. Someone enquiring with the Captain, relaying news, following the rules. There would've been more."

"So, what do you suggest we do? Things are wrong, where do we go from here?"

"We don't have all that long before we have to be back."

"Either we go back now and share what we've found, or more accurately, not found, or we keep looking for an explanation."

"Keep looking." She said after a moment of consideration. "We have time to head over to the dining hall, see who's there, scan the rooms on the way, hopefully find something useful."

"Sounds good to me." I lied. I wanted to go back. I didn't tell her that though, I couldn't bring myself to. She wouldn't understand.

She led the way. We gradually picked up the pace, maybe we weren't as thorough as we should have been, but there was just no one. No cleaners, no pedestrians, no maintenance, we even passed an active work zone.

There should've been two electricians fixing the wiring in a checkpoint station, and yet the area was completely empty. Their tools were present, but they were not. We didn't linger for long. They'd broken protocol and we had to assume it was for a good reason.

We were jogging by the time we reached the dining hall, each empty room spurred us faster, but we had to be smart about it, sprinting would've been dumb, even though it would've helped release the tension coiling in my muscles.

Avery paused outside the door. I didn't even know it had a door, I'd certainly never seen it closed. It was a bad sign and yet there was a comfort to it as well. It was easier to reason that the quietness stemmed from it being closed. It was the perfect opportunity to indulge in denial. If the door stayed closed everything would remain perfectly ordinary. At least, I had no way of knowing otherwise.

"Ready?" She asked, she was stalling. Hand poised, shaking slightly, waiting for reassurance.

"No." I replied, reaching my hand to hers and forcing us both to get it over with.

All we could do was stand there and watch. I was wrong, kind of. The door didn't need to stay closed for the other side to remain normal. As soon as it slid open, the familiar noise reached us. There was chatting, and walking, clattering of utensils, and shoes scraping against the floor.

Avery closed the door.

The quietness that followed was heavy, it was fundamentally wrong and logistically impossible and yet it kept happening. She opened and closed it again, normality resumed and was instantly cut off, as if everything just paused as soon as we stopped witnessing it.

She opened it and stepped through.

I watched her hand fly to her face, covering her mouth. Her

legs buckled and she instinctively reached for the wall with her other hand. It barely made contact before she flinched away, horror consuming her expression as she stared at the spot she touched. She fell to the floor and wretched as one of the normal people walked through her.

I couldn't look away. I couldn't move. Everything was normal except for Avery and everyone's refusal to acknowledge her presence. She was calling to me, I could see her mouth moving but there was no appropriate sound, nothing that matched up with it, just the regular hustle of a room full of people.

I stepped into the room and saw what had caused that reaction from her.

The smell hit me as soon as I crossed the threshold, the putrid smell of death and rotting flesh. There were no bodies, there couldn't be, not with how much blood and viscera decorated the walls. There were entrails and various... Substances littering the floor and furniture. I wasn't willing to look close enough to identify any of it. I glanced and that was bad enough.

My focus shifted to Avery as soon as I could convince my brain to look away. I needed to get her out, I needed to get her away, some place safe. She was gently weeping and for a moment that was all I cared about.

I coaxed her to her feet, guiding her back to the hallway, blocking her view when she tried to look back. I didn't let her see it. I closed the door on the normal room to prevent her from seeing the exact moment it stopped being normal and turned into the mess we had just seen. I wasn't quick enough to block out the first of the screams.

"What was that?" Her voice was broken, strained and scared.

"I don't know. We need to get back. The Captain needs to know." I pulled her arm, leading her back the way we had originally come.

"And tell him what exactly? None of that happened. That wasn't real. It couldn't be."

"Then we tell him we hallucinated. Come on."

She shook me off and followed, accepting what I said, though clearly reluctantly.

The door thudded. I picked up speed. It banged. I grabbed Avery and we shifted into a run. It splintered and the screams broke through. We sprinted.

The floor rattled with each thundering footstep as it got bigger and closer and stronger. I peered back, our running meant nothing, the dining hall was right behind us the whole way, no matter how far we got.

Their screams echoed over and over and I almost saw a flash of whatever it was. Almost.

A body flew through us. A crew member overtook us. The lights flickered, leaving a questionable smear across the wall and no body in sight.

We rounded a corner and the cockpit came into view. I pulled Avery close to me as something flitted past the edge of our eyesight and destroyed the exact spot she'd been occupying.

I didn't dare look back. I knew it would be in full view by now but I couldn't bring myself to do it. Everything was forward, our way to the safety of the next room was forward, and there was no need to look back.

Maybe she was just braver than me.

She looked. She broke free from my grasp and she looked and she screamed. It extended for an uncomfortable amount of time, longer than I ever thought possible, before ceasing. The sudden silence was almost as painful.

I had to look then. I had to look at what was left of her, what was splattered along the corridor. Some of it got on my clothes.

I had to keep going. I didn't want to. My body didn't give me a choice. I crashed into the cockpit and fell to the floor.

"What is the meaning of this?" He saw my face and nothing

else, tearing his eyes away from his screen long enough to put a name to a face, but no longer.

I panted hard. My whole body shook. My voice was stuck in my throat.

"I meant 30 minutes, not 30 seconds."

The door thudded.

"Get back out there and do your job."

It banged.

I stood up and he finally looked at me.

"What happened to you? Where's Avery?"

All I could do was shake my head as the door splintered and the screams broke through and everything was plunged into darkness.

There was a click. Then another. And another. A moment passed. Then there was light.

MY NEW HOME

Sam

I thought it was a dreadful idea. Our relationship had been rocky for a while and then suddenly he was all lovey-dovey and confusing and demanding the next step in commitment. I didn't want to move in with him. I didn't have the financials for it and relying on him was scary. But I loved him. That's what he kept telling me. I loved him, so I had to take that step with him.

If I refused then that meant I didn't love him and I'd been using him the whole time. I wasn't some lying whore who was just taking advantage of him, and I had to prove it. So, I moved in with him.

We started small, my lease ended so I just stayed at his while we looked for somewhere more permanent. It was the best our relationship had been in a very long time. Sure, I felt uncomfortable at first, but he eased all my concerns.

I was there for two months and we had a date night each week, he lit candles, dressed up nice, even cooked for me. Everything he did reminded me of the man I'd fallen in love with to begin with. It was truly delightful while it lasted.

Soon enough he'd found his dream home. He could comfortably afford it, it was an easy drive to his work, and in a great school district. He brought it before I even knew the place existed.

He was saving me the stress. Only one of us needed to carry it, he was in charge of everything so that burden fell on him and I should have been grateful. Admittedly, he was impressively efficient at getting it all sorted.

I knew there was no reason for me to feel weird about it all, things were rocky and then he did what he could to make amends. That's how relationships work. Not that he had anything to make amends for, he never did anything wrong. Everything was my fault, I understood that just as well as he did.

And yet he offered me this opportunity. I'd never done anything to deserve it and all I could offer him was shitty feelings and uncertainty. I didn't tell him that. I hinted at times, hesitated in my responses and avoided direct answers. After all, it wouldn't have been very loving of me to start arguments at such times. He didn't need that added stress. I didn't either.

I was trapped in the obligation. I know that was an awful way to think of it, but that's how I felt. There was just no way out of it. I was constantly making mistakes and hurting him and that is what he asked of me to fix it all. I had to fix it. That was my job, after all. Fix my messes. He did everything he could to make it easy for me.

He handed me my own key. He let me choose which room would be the best bedroom, which would be the best place for his office, how to decorate it all. I used to be an interior designer before him, it was so much fun getting to use those skills again. Plus, the house was hideous so there was an awful lot to do.

The place was functional which was a relief. The kitchen clearly hadn't been designed with convenience in mind, but it was useable at the very least. Unfortunately, that was low priority, he was never in the kitchen and I could make do so there was no need to improve it.

His office was first, he didn't spend much time in there but when he did it was during meetings. The place had to be presentable, visually acceptable for his colleagues and clients. He was a high value worker and it was necessary to show that in his surroundings. So, the office was first.

All the decisions had to be run through him. Ultimately, he was in charge of any actual purchases, but the designing went smooth enough. He seemed pleased with my original design idea, it was classy and comfortable and a massive upgrade compared to his last place. It ticked all of his boxes so I got started as soon as I could.

He bought everything I asked for. He cleared the room, brought in all the equipment I'd need, and left me to it. I got started just as he was leaving for work.

The first layer of paint went quicker than I expected, the day was lovely and warm and it had dried in time for me to start a second coat just as he was arriving home. I yelled a "hello", a "how are you", a "foods in the oven", and then I did the unforgivable.

I spilled the paint.

I dread to think how much worse it would have been without the ground sheets. It was bad enough and I didn't even ruin anything. I tried to clean it up without him noticing but the silent tears took their toll, my face was all red and puffy by the time he came to check my progress.

The mess was gone but I couldn't lie. I'd wasted his resources, I didn't care about his money, how much he had to work to achieve this dream, how I was out to ruin this for him. I don't remember specifically what was said but it was loud and scary.

He was always a lot more expressive with his arms when he was angry, his movements all bigger and faster, more jarring. The walls were wet and I couldn't risk knocking the ladder over. He was between me and the door and all I could do was stand there. He never hit me but there were times when I got in his way. This was one of those times.

His forearm connected with my shoulder and the front door slammed shut. His whole body whipped towards to the noise. It was the other side of the house. He didn't say anything else. He just quietly, tensely, walked out of the room and through to the main hallway. I didn't follow and he didn't come back. I think he went out into the garden for a bit.

I made sure to finish up the painting. I couldn't risk falling behind schedule. I was just sort of waiting for him to blame me. I'd left windows open all over the house, between the general musty smell of the place and the paint fumes, I needed the air flow. I probably hadn't been careful enough with the door and broken the latch so when he got home it didn't catch properly. The breeze could have pushed it open and then all that air flow slammed it closed.

That sounded like the most logical explanation. It was all perfectly plausible. I decided he was waiting for me to admit to it, to let me keep my dignity through the process. It was better for me to acknowledge my wrongdoings than it was for him to seek out an apology.

I found him outside, fiddling with something beside the front door. I knew better than to ask questions. I'd rehearsed what I wanted to say, planned the words and practised the tone. I didn't get it perfect, but it was sufficient. He gently cupped my face, tenderly stroked the tears off of my cheek, and kissed me on the forehead.

All was forgiven. As long as I took more care going forward. Another mistake like that would not be forgiven. Another mistake like that would have to be punished. He pulled me in for a hug. And that was it. Conflict over. The evening could proceed as normal. And it did.

He updated me on how his day went, his work ventures and stresses, his plans for the following day. He let me know the deadline for his office had changed, it needed to be ready by his next meeting. I had three days instead of the week I was promised. He knew it was inconvenient and he was ever so sorry, but there was nothing he could do. This was something he needed from me. My own job would have to be put on pause for a bit.

I couldn't really say no, not after how badly I'd messed up with the paint. I know he said all was forgiven but I also knew I needed to redeem myself somehow. He was offering me another opportunity. I should have been grateful.

Technically he was my boss's boss, so I knew I'd be able to get the time off without issue. It was a lot of work I didn't want to be rushing, though. I'd got the bulk of the painting done, there was still the accents and any touch ups, all of which would need time to dry, then getting the furniture in and set up in the right place, and then the decorating.

He wanted plants, ornaments, his certificates to take pride of place on the centre wall. I needed to frame and hang them. That in itself was going to take a fair bit of work. I had to get it all ready before asking for permission to use his tools and I had to time the actual work for when he was going to be out. He didn't like the noise.

I got it done, though. It felt impossible, right up until that final finishing touch when I could breathe again. The last of his certificates were hung and I could show off my hard work. It was exactly how I'd planned it, exactly what he'd approved. There was no reason he wouldn't like it.

I was still nervous, of course. I always took so much pride in my work and it's normal to be nervous when sharing something so personal. It didn't mean anything. I wanted him to like it, that was all.

He assured me he did. He promised me he loved it, he was ever so proud of what I'd done. He was so pleased he'd be able to look good in front of his clients. He even treated me to a fancy date and cooked me dinner which was ever so kind of him. And unexpected. I knew better than to expect anything like that.

True to his word, the meeting was an important one. It set him up nicely with his clients, a big business deal was made, one that would keep him out of town for a couple weeks. It was an opportunity for us both, he could prove himself to some potential long term clients and network in a thriving city, and I could focus on the house.

I planned as much as I could before he left, got his seal of approval for everything. He even let me borrow one of his credit cards with free reign to buy what I needed. He would check, of course. He always checked.

I couldn't go wild, but it was more freedom than I'd had in quite a while. It was exciting. I didn't have to worry about making noise, about being in the way, or any of those things. I could just exist in the house, doing what I wanted when I wanted. Oh, it was wonderful.

I still hated the place, but being able to open a window and put some music on at the same time was great. And I could even sing along. And dance! I didn't have to care how I looked. I could wear the worst outfit I could manage and prance about.

That couple of weeks passed by far too quickly. I got so much work done and had so much fun and before I knew it, my final day had arrived. I had to dedicate it to making the place ready for him.

I'd left some of my stuff in shared spaces, the kitchen was far from spotless, and most of the windows blissfully open. I had to set all of it right. I had to check and double check that I hadn't missed anything, and then I had to get to work. He couldn't know I'd had fun.

Honestly, I was dreading his return. I know that was awful of me. I loved him. I should have been excited to see him again. I should have missed him and moped around during his absence. I did everything wrong while he was gone, and I had to hide all of that as best as I could.

I left my blanket on the back of the couch. It blended in so well and I didn't think and it was one of the first things he noticed.

His trip hadn't gone well, his journey had been plagued with delays and diversions, he was in a foul mood when he got back and I added fuel to that. I'd been careless and hadn't thought about him adequately.

I should have known better than to leave the house in such a state when all he wanted to do was sit back and relax and now he couldn't do that. I'd ruined his evening before it had even begun.

This time he did slap me. I wanted to offer him a hug, some form of comfort. He was a physical contact kind of guy and I thought I was offering him what he wanted. I was wrong. I touched him without his consent so he returned the favour.

It was what I deserved. He yelled it at me. Over and over and I just stood there and sobbed. Then he yelled at me about that. I was making too much noise. He wanted a quiet evening and I was being selfishly loud.

He grabbed me and shook me and I felt my body flying backwards out of his grasp. I was flung through the kitchen, around the corner, and into the utility room. The door slammed behind me and that set him off more.

He was screaming and stomping and crashing around as he followed me, demanding I open the door before he opened it. He would make me pay if he had to open it.

Except, he couldn't. It didn't have a lock and had been loose in the frame and yet nothing he did worked. No amount of throwing his weight around, slamming his fists, kicking the handle out, could get it to open. The flimsy wood held strong.

Someone walking past must have heard the commotion, phoned the police. At some point they turned up, sirens blaring. He was smart enough to shut up before they parked up. He fed them some bullshit about how I was trapped in the utility room and he was panicking trying to free me. I think they believed him.

They helped him take the hinges off, I'd definitely left a screwdriver somewhere easy for them to find and between them they made quick work of it. The door slipped out if its frame and I was pulled to my feet and into a suffocating hug.

He was saying about how worried he'd been, how he'd thought I must have fallen and blocked the doorway, how relieved he was that I was fine and well. He thanked them profusely, asked how he could make it up to them. They smiled and shared how pleased they were it had all worked out.

Standard protocol because of the statement of whoever phoned them, along with the bruise on my cheek, meant they had to offer me the option of escalating. One of them handed me a card with his details, the other explained that since it was a domestic dispute, it wasn't something they were willing to get involved in. Not unless I was going to press charges, which was ridiculous of course. There was a lot of contradiction in what they said but ultimately it was clear I was wasting their time.

He didn't speak to me for days after that. We co-existed in silence and tension until he was ready to forgive me. It wasn't my fault the door had jammed, he had to accept that eventually. I shouldn't have run away either, I shouldn't have been in a position where I could get trapped like that.

Once his anger had passed, he was ready to comment on the decorating. I'd done a spectacular job on most of it. He had some criticisms, of course, he hadn't been as involved like with his office, so it wasn't all to his tastes. Nothing that wasn't fixable with a bit of effort. He made sure to steer me right.

It was good to have him back. I hated having to tiptoe around his moods, I could barely stand to be in the same room as him when he got like that. He was a black-hole, sucking in all the energy in the place.

One of his criticisms was in regard to the window on the landing. He kept finding it open, no matter how many times he closed it. He'd noticed it during his silence, so had I.

I thought he was trying to set me up, find a reason to yell at me, but apparently he caught me closing it enough times he decided it wasn't me opening it. I didn't know he'd been paying that much attention to me, I was glad he had, I didn't want to get accused.

Instead we got to share the confusion. Neither of us understood how it kept happening, it didn't look like the kind of window that could break in that way, if such a thing even existed. Clearly we were wrong.

Clearly it was just broken in a way that caught the wind, or a mechanism slipped funky, a spring sprung, I don't know. I never paid that much attention to how windows worked. That was the installer's job.

Whatever it was, it was driving him crazy. It kept him busy and out of my way while he hired men to fix it. Multiple men from multiple companies, each with the same results. There was nothing they could do. They tried to explain they didn't know how to fix something that wasn't broken.

He was insistent so they offered placation. Or, more likely, they played him for his money. He was desperate they did something, and so they did. They checked the seal, oiled the hinges, messed around with some screws, nothing made any difference.

He gave up on the idea of fixing it, next was replacement. It wouldn't open if it couldn't. The people he hired tried to explain how it was a risk closing off such a prominent escape route if there was a fire or other such emergency, but he was adamant. He did not want that window opening ever again, but he did still want a window there, so they got to work.

He was in such a good mood once they were done. Practically walking around with a skip in his step. It didn't last long. He had a meeting that same evening, another make-or-break deal. He was confident and proud walking into that meeting. He was bitter and angry when he walked out.

I met him with food, I was taking it to his office in what I thought was a loving gesture while he was busy. He stormed out and found me in the hallway. He sneered something about how I was trying to ruin his career by interrupting him, how selfish and ungrateful I was for all his hard work. He snatched the meal away from me and slammed it into the wall.

The smash of the plate coincided exactly with the smash of the window. Less than twelve hours after it had been installed. I'd have been pleased if I hadn't been so scared. We were nowhere near it. The glass flew outwards. With force.

With so much force, the glass scattered across our garden and nothing we could find could have caused it. The front door was locked, nobody could have gotten in to cause such damage. That mystery distracted him for a while, until the next one occurred.

And there was a next one, and several after that. All with logical explanations, he yelled at me as his phone flew out of his hand. We weren't being haunted, I was insane for suggesting such a thing, he shouted as every single cupboard door opened. Nothing was going on, it was a normal house and nothing abnormal was going on, he screamed moments before his body was yanked sideways and out of the front door. It locked behind him.

That went on, very obvious incidents becoming increasingly frequent until they were daily occurrences and impossible to ignore. Every time he fixed that window it broke the same day until he just stopped fixing it.

Every time he went to hit me, one of us was pulled away. every time he raised his voice, slammed something, broke something, an even louder crashing noise was heard.

It was all in my head. He made sure to tell me that every time. The book he threw was still on the floor where it landed, it was crazy of me to think a book could put itself away. The glass he broke was still broken, there was nothing on the counter top. He'd walked calmly to the door and locked it behind him as he left, I didn't need to let him in, he had his keys the whole time and just wanted to go for a walk.

Whatever I thought had happened definitely hadn't. It didn't matter what I thought, it definitely couldn't have been that. I was losing my mind. I was imagining things. I needed professional help. I couldn't mention any of it to anyone because they'd have me locked up. I believed him.

He decided what I needed was a day out of the house and he had the perfect opportunity for me. It was my birthday. It was the only time I was allowed to visit my parents so I spent the day there.

We took pictures upon my arrival. My ma posted them immediately after taking them. We sat in their garden enjoying cake and lemonade and I made sure not to mention any of what was going on. I never mentioned any of it. I'd learnt that a long time ago.

My old friends showed up unexpectedly, invited by my parents on the condition they kept it secret. He couldn't find out. That was their gift to me, they knew physical gifts were pointless so they found an alternative.

They all snuck in. Anyone watching from the road wouldn't have known a thing. They showed their support, something I hadn't experienced in such a long time. I hadn't felt so loved in such a long time.

I was only allowed to spend a few hours there, but I just wasn't ready to leave. I turned my phone off once the messages started. Imani noticed, she used to be my closest friend, she always noticed.

Out of everyone, she kept in contact with me the longest. Even after I stopped replying. She stayed close with my parents the whole time, she helped get everyone together. And then, when it was time to leave, she offered to drive me home. I couldn't afford to be out any longer than I had to be. It was a long walk, after all, and I was going to be in more than enough trouble, so I accepted.

She was going to drop me off just around the corner. That was the plan until we spotted the police cars. She refused to leave me until we knew what was going on. She walked up to the police officers with me. They asked us both questions, who we were, where we were coming from, how we knew the man who lived there. All perfectly easy to answer honestly.

That's when they broke the news. A colleague had visited, an arranged meeting. When nobody answered the door, she got suspicious, used the spare key around back and let herself in.

She'd found him there, splayed out on the floor, and immediately called an ambulance. It was pointless. They were far too late to do anything. She knew we were going through troubles and she'd shared as much, I was a prime suspect until I showed up.

She left just before we'd arrived. We arrived just in time to clear my name. It couldn't have been me. I had been out all day. My alibi was solid, picture evidence and all. That's when I became a grief stricken partner, in their eyes and I was assured there was nothing I could have done differently.

It had been a tragic accident, they told me. A trip down the stairs while he was doing laundry. The basket blocking his view, hands occupied, it could happen to anyone, they told me.

He'd never done laundry in his life. I wasn't about to tell them that. I also wasn't grief stricken. I wasn't going to tell them that either. My tears weren't from grief, they were relief. I was free. I wasn't crazy and I was free.

The worst thing that ever happened to me somehow ended up being the best thing that ever happened to me. I liked my new home. I don't think I'd ever felt so safe before.

A SLOW EXTINCTION

Amir

It took a while for anyone to notice. Shit happens, right? Tragedies occur, people get hurt, kids sometimes just kind of sound like they're getting murdered. You know, screams happen. Sure, when it does it catches your attention, but it's just a part of life.

Unexplained deaths aren't really all that uncommon either. First they have to be found, there's so much empty space in the world, so many locked doors, and so many people who would go unmissed. That's just another part of life, some people vanish and that's it, they're just gone.

Then they have to actually look beyond surface level, and sometimes there's just no point. Why subject someone to all that testing when by all accounts they died because of a car accident? Or old age, or that terminal illness they'd been fighting for so long, or any other seemingly obvious reason? You don't look for something when you don't know there's something to look for. You do the bare minimum standard procedure and you move on.

It averaged about 10 people every second. That's 864,000 deaths a day. It sounds like a lot, it feels like a lot, but that was global. When it started there was probably around 9 billion people, about 350,000 deaths was normal, and we weren't exactly short on war and famine and natural disasters and whatever. We already knew that number was going up anyway. Honestly, it's amazing how many people can die before it's considered a problem.

Plus, when a local homeless man starts screaming and

clutching at his face, he was just a weirdo who died of a drug overdose. When a local off-grid camper doesn't come home when expected, it's sad but that's the risk you take with that kind of activity.

But when it's the pretty blonde waitress at that popular café everyone goes to, it's the talk of the town for months. She was young and healthy and it was a mystery that needed solving. Except it didn't get solved, not really. She was young and healthy and there was nothing wrong with her. So, they made something up.

It was a stress related blood clot that went undetected, that's what they told us, that can happen sometimes. Something to do with birth control maybe. That's also just a thing that happens sometimes.

The power of hindsight makes it pretty clear that wasn't what actually happened, but it was so easy to believe at the time. And she was one of the first, we didn't know anything unusual was going on. We couldn't know.

Rumours that something was up started spreading, but it was just that for a while, everyone knew someone who knew someone who'd died the same way. But nobody knew for sure that it was the same way.

And then it became an easy scapegoat, people in denial about the actual circumstances of their loved ones death could claim to be a part of this mystery. There was a solidarity in that particular grief that was shared far easier. It was a worldwide community problem, not just a personal one.

It somehow validated and invalidated the situation. It made it far harder to keep track of, but people started believing it more readily. And when people believed it, they noticed it. We had some incredible tech and none of it mattered, it was the belief that led to progress.

Once people started to believe, the deaths become more

frequent. I didn't understand it at the time, I thought it was just awareness that made it look like it was happening more. When you look, you see. If you don't look then you can't see. It got to the point where everyone was looking, so of course a lot more could get noticed.

That awareness spread the belief. It was an important factor but it wasn't the deciding one. People spent a lot of time trying to figure out what that was, what connected all of these seemingly random deaths.

They weren't random, though. They were picked. They were loyal. There was an unspoken threshold that they had all surpassed. A criteria that eventually billions of people met.

It wasn't everyone, and it wasn't all at once, but it was enough and chaos ensued. Birth rates weren't picking up the slack, in fact they were falling as people got scared. Humanity was dropping like flies.

Government officials, secret spies, people who had very important jobs that couldn't easily be replaced were dropping dead across the globe. There were assassination accusals and threats of nukes. A handful of very important people were making very important decisions that the rest of us were terrified of.

Humanity's fear was going to be its doom. Most of us had known that for quite some time, except then it had been a distant thing. A 'one day' kind of knowing. We didn't expect that day to be imminent.

Or rather, days. Because humanity did persevere. War broke out, a worldwide issue resulted in a worldwide war. Nobody could blame it on anybody so nobody knew who to target, that made everybody fair game.

It became so hard to keep faith throughout it. To watch atrocities and still believe... I don't know how we did it. Those of us that survived it all, I mean.

There were times when we faltered, it was only human to

do so, there was no shame in that. I definitely struggled with it more than some. That's probably why I was one of the last. It was exhausting at times, to be stuck with the remnants of humanity, to be surviving the worst things we'd ever had to survive.

But I held out, through it all, I survived, and I maintained my belief. Its foundations were rocky but as soon as I realised how important it was, I put in the work, I fixed the wobbles and holes it had accumulated. I dedicated myself.

I tried to spread the word. Those missionaries, preachers, whoever, always annoyed me so I was careful not to push like that. I sowed the seeds and hoped those who I was leaving behind would be able to find their way with me.

It wasn't about the specifics, it never was. It was about honest commitment, genuine belief, not shrouded in control or fear or hatred. In whatever way that looked for every individual, whether to the self or the whole because ultimately there was no difference.

And then it was my turn. I saw it. I saw everything all at once. I was everything all at once. And they were there, standing before me, one finger gently resting against my forehead, wings encompassing us both in an embrace. I had a choice to make and I did. I made the exact same choice as everyone else. I was ready.

2744

Violet

A hiss of decompressing air, a whir of moving mechanical parts, three shrill beeps. I shouldn't have been awake to hear any of that, I shouldn't have felt a sudden rush of warmth, nor watched the door to my pod slip open. At that point, I couldn't know that, though.

I was awake, my pod was open, we must have arrived so I went through the procedure. Deep breaths. Name, Violet. Age, 21. Destination, planet 24-6-C, or colloquially known as Azura. What else was there? Occupation? Next of kin? A handful of other uncomfortably formal facts I was supposed to list off?

We were told it would ease the disorientation, told by people who had never experienced it. I was pretty sure it was making it worse. Thinking was confusing, but moving, now that was something I could manage. Starting small, of course, long-term sleep took its toll on the body, after all.

Except my body was fine, strong even. Stronger than it had been before I left, perhaps? That was ridiculous, of course. Standing definitely felt different, the way my body held itself up was wrong, there was far more muscle and tension than I remembered. But I was still disorientated, that was all it was, surely?

A handful of people were awake for the full voyage, we were told they would be there to welcome us, to keep the ship running smoothly and fix whatever needed fixing, if the need arose. It wouldn't, of course, this was a high-tech ship, nothing would go wrong, the people were just another of the many fail safes in place.

Waking up was supposed to be staggered over a couple weeks, there was a timetable, it was all planned. The first group would get some time to adjust and then everyone would go and greet someone from the next group, they'd then get a couple days to adjust and then move on to the next group. So on and so forth until everyone was awake, and then decent would occur. It was all outlined in our contract.

I expected to be part of the fifth group, somewhere in the middle of the timetable. I expected people to be milling about, maybe crossing paths in hallways. Not busy, but not desolate either.

I was greeted by no-one. I crossed paths with no-one. All of the pods around me were closed.

A defect perhaps? The easy assumption was that mine had opened early, a one in a million possibility, if even that. We were all warned about it, to ease our concerns more than anything else. Just go find some of the awake crew, easy enough.

We'd been shown a map, shown which pod room we would be in, what floor that would be on, where the nearest points of interest were. I wasn't confident in my ability to remember it all accurately, but it was something I could work with, if nothing else. A communal room, not too far off, somewhere to aim for. It was a big ship, though, and I was thoroughly disorientated.

A ten minute peruse, perhaps. I wasn't in any rush, I wanted to find people and that involved looking, but it felt like an awful lot longer. I don't know if I reached the communal room I was thinking of, but I did find a man sat at a table, back to me, head in his hands.

"Oh good, hi, I think my pod opened early?"

He didn't move.

"Can you help me?" I moved towards him, towards where I assumed his line of sight was, towards a space where I could get a better view of him and the pool of blood at his feet.

I was vaguely aware of my body getting nauseous, though it was a far off feeling, much in the same way that the metallic smell in the air was far off. I could have noticed it if I wanted to but goddamn did I not want to.

I didn't want to look at him. I didn't want to see the three slashes in his body, across his chest. Whatever had done this had gone clean through the muscle, showing the mangled ribs, deflated lungs, and absent heart. I didn't want to notice the 2742 written elegantly on the table in front of him. I didn't know what was worse, the possibility that a human could do this, or the possibility that they couldn't.

I also didn't want to throw up, but much like everything else, I didn't have any real choice in the matter. Once that was out of my system, the adrenaline kicked in.

The idea that whoever, or perhaps whatever, had done this could still be around hit me hard and very suddenly. I didn't run, though my body ached to do so. Somewhere in my brain it had clicked that I probably didn't want to be making too much noise.

I used to be religious, I used to believe in the importance of preparing a body for the afterlife. I desperately wanted to offer him that. I also desperately wanted to run and hide and never think about it ever again. He wasn't the first dead body I'd seen. He was, by far, the worst.

I just left him there. I didn't know who he was. I couldn't honour him in the way he deserved. There was no way of saving him, nothing I could do. It still felt wrong, though. The weight of this strangers demise was heavy, there was a grief to it that I didn't understand, couldn't understand. I'd lost people I was close with before, I was familiar with that feeling, I wasn't familiar with experiencing it towards someone I'd never met before.

I needed a plan. I couldn't wander aimlessly, it had become abundantly clear that wasn't a safe option. I couldn't just do nothing either, be a sitting duck during God knows what kind of disaster I'd found myself in. The pods were the only place my scrambled brain could come up with, so back to the pods I went.

A combination of my increased urgency and decreased meandering meant my walk back went much quicker. The entrance came into view at roughly the same time I realised my hearing aid was picking up on some static.

It started subtly, just on the edge of my hearing, but gradually got louder as I kept walking. It sounded like electrical interference, almost like one of the old antique radios I used to play with with my brother. The hearing aid I wore back then was considerably less advanced, but then so was the radio we'd acquired.

A comms system, perhaps? I hadn't heard it earlier so I figured maybe someone was trying to get a message out, maybe they were looking for other people like me. Obviously I had to find it. It gave me something to do.

Each pod room had a control room, somewhere they could use to keep an eye on whether everything was functioning properly and then open them up when the time came. Somewhere that would have been by far smarter for me to try and locate earlier, had I remembered it existed.

I couldn't remember where it had been on the map but logically it must have been somewhere near the entrance of the pod room, somewhere near where I was. It wasn't the first door I looked in, but it didn't take too many tries, luckily.

The static noise grew as I got closer until I found myself in a computer room and it was the only thing I could hear. So, in I went.

There were a few desks with computers on, a handful of screens that showed various angles of the pods, regularly flicking through different wide angle camera feeds. I didn't pay too much attention to those, I wanted a comms system, not a surveillance system. Plus one of them was faulty anyway, the video was all distorted and funky.

THE START OF YOUR NEW LIFE

It briefly occurred to me that whatever fault had caused that distortion might have been causing the interference in my hearing aid, but I was too set on the comms idea so I set my sights on one of the nearby desks, settling into the chair.

There was a small communication device, which was basically the next best thing, an ear cuff that I slipped around my non-staticky ear and then promptly dropped when it offered me that same uncomfortable noise.

So I switched my attention to the computer. The user interface was clearly designed for convenience. It had turned on when I had sat down and looked like diagnostic software, or at least that was what came to mind when I looked at it.

There were 5 cryo-pod rooms on each floor, 1,000 pods in each, 100 floors so 500,000 passengers in total. That's what I remembered being told, and the computer seemed to be showing me information for 1,000 of them. 20 rows of 50. A computer tab for each row. It was simple enough.

I looked through all of them and found four open pods, or at least four pods with error signals that I assumed meant they were open. It felt like a fair assumption to make especially as one of the error signals matched roughly where I felt my pod would have been.

I clicked on it, on the error message. A video feed popped up, a shot of an open and empty pod. My name was written across the top of the page, beneath it a photo, the picture of me that had been taken for my ID, and then some of my relevant demographic information. The bottom of the page was what interested me.

Error detected, 00:00. Code, unknown. Fix, unknown. Contact, unknown.

It didn't fill me with confidence. I couldn't know what any of it meant and the static was only getting louder. I couldn't think but I needed to. I looked away from the computer, I needed a moment away from the information, a perspective shift per se, so I glanced up at the camera feeds again. The faulty feed had moved to a different screen and I realised I needed to do the same.

I closed out of my pod's information and clicked onto one of the others. A new feed popped up, the same errors and unknowns as mine, except this one showed an open and empty pod with the number 1365 written elegantly across the glass. It was the same shade of red, the same cursive style, as I had seen in front of the stranger earlier. I clicked over to a new pod before I could think about it.

This next one was like mine, open, empty, and absent of any numbers. Someone was awake like me. Marco Cipriani. Error detected, 00:23. Code, unknown. Fix, unknown. Contact, unknown. A full price passenger.

Most of the people on this voyage paid. They filled the crew slots first, offered a 'reduced fee' to colony workers, then hiked the price right up for the tourists. I didn't fit into any of those categories. I was a guinea-pig.

The general consensus was that you couldn't send people like me on voyages like this. Technology implanted in the brain often didn't mix well with cryo-sleep. But this was new tech, designed specifically to overcome that problem. So they paid me to go on the trip. It was also part of the deal to upgrade my hearing aid and the attached brain implant, to make sure the tech worked as intended.

My last one worked fine, though I wasn't overly fond of the cold brain feeling during winter and the occasional glitch. I always thought that was just what having an implant would be like, that I'd have to tolerate it if I wanted my brain to work like it used to.

Then I got the fancy new one, it was wonderful and for the first time since getting it, I didn't want it any more. Hell, for the first time since getting my hearing aid as a kid, I didn't want to hear anything any more

I didn't want to hear the gradual increase in static directly into my head, I didn't want to hear the metal vibration in my brain, I didn't want to hear what I could only assume was the scream of someone dying.

The noise and sensations in my head were getting increasingly intense, it had been manageable until the scream ended and the static hiked up into a roar. It went from uncomfortable to painful to debilitating, my vision blurred and caved in as my body slumped out of the chair and onto the floor. I wasn't awake long enough to feel the impact.

I don't know how long I was unconscious for. I didn't immediately get up either, I stayed put while the pain subsided and my vision returned to normal. The surveillance screens were just within view from where I lay, just enough to see the faulty feed on yet another different screen.

The computer layout was designed for convenience but the surveillance sure wasn't, I couldn't even begin to figure out the pattern the screens were on. There wasn't any logic to where the distorted one ended up. I quickly got bored of trying to make sense of it and picked myself back up.

Marco's pod video was still up, only now, instead of looking like my own, it had an elegantly written 2743 across the glass. I sat with that for a moment, letting the weight of those numbers hit me, a weight I'd danced with earlier but hadn't really solidified. 2743 dead?

I closed out of it and looked back up at the main camera screens. I let them play out, looking for a distraction more than anything else. The lack of any distortion barely even registered in my still somewhat scrambled brain.

What did register was the body, propped up against the wall and framed perfectly centred for the camera facing it. Or maybe the camera had been moved to perfectly frame the body, after all, I don't think any of the other cameras faced empty walls.

Those same three slashes were across his chest, the same writing, damn near the same number, even.

2743. The number that had been written on Marco's pod was also written across the wall. I had no intention of looking close enough to see if the faces matched, it didn't feel necessary, the hair was the same and that was as much as I cared to analyse.

There was a horror to witnessing such a thing, though the distance this time was through a screen. I couldn't smell it, I couldn't see the details, I was just assuming it would all be the same as the other guy. There was a hint of curiosity, to go and see just how similar the injuries were, but the desire to do literally anything else easily won out.

There wasn't any grief this time. I didn't care for Marco, not on a personal level. It was a community loss and I felt that but mostly it felt weird to know this strangers name, but not the name of the last guy. It felt wrong somehow. Like a betrayal almost, as if I was forgetting the name of a childhood friend.

Not that he was that, of course, I'd never met him before. I'd never met either of them. I should have felt the same for both of them, surely?

The camera feed changed to a far more normal scene and I'd set my mind on my next task. I owed him a name.

Five pod rooms per floor, he wasn't from any of the open ones in this room, so it had to be one of the other four. Adding other floors into the equation was a complication I wasn't in the mood to factor in, so I didn't. I just pulled up a map, found the next nearest room, and did my best to memorise a route.

I managed to get there without too much trouble, all things considered. I got lucky with finding the first pod control room, I knew more or less where I was going and my misguided theory about the static seemed to get me where I needed. I didn't encounter any static this time, nor any screams or bodies, much to my relief.

It was a stressful walk, nonetheless. I knew something was out there. I didn't know what, where, or how many. I didn't want those questions answered either. Any other situation and it would have been a perfectly pleasant walk, I even found signs that pointed me in the right direction.

This one had six open pods, all with the same errors and unknowns, four of them had numbers written across them but none were his. So I pulled up a map and looked for the next one.

It was only as I neared the third pod room that I started to doubt whether I was making the right choice. I could have been doing something useful, what exactly, I didn't know, but something. So I justified it, I was looking for answers, I was looking for people, I was looking for an idea on what I needed to do to survive.

I did find some of those things.

The third room also had six open pods, three with numbers. The second one I clicked was his. It showed me a picture of his face, considerably cleaner shaven, his name, Aeden Lynn, and a camera feed to his pod. 2742 was written as expected, except below it sat a woman. There was a rush of familiarity, of warmth and comfort, though I couldn't find any context to warrant such feelings towards her.

Obviously I had to talk to her. Obviously that was absolutely terrifying and I was torn between a desperate need for comfort and a desperate need to understand what it was exactly that I was feeling. There was almost a relief amidst the mundanity of such anxiety, I'd seen mutilated corpses but talking to someone was where I drew the line. Or maybe I'd just ran out of adrenaline.

I found her on the main camera feeds, found a way to stop the screen from switching to a different view. I watched her briefly between skimming through the data of the rest of the open pods. They all had the same errors and unknowns, all of them opened at 00:00. Except Marco. I couldn't connect the dots on my own, I had to go and talk to her. I took one last look at Aeden, at his name and his face, to honour his death in the only way I felt I could, before I once again left him.

She wasn't hard to find, there were twenty rows of pods, it was fifty-fifty, left or right, and then just look down the row until I spotted the only other person in the room. I tried to make my footsteps as audible as I could without becoming threatening. I wanted to make noise so I wouldn't spook her by just turning up, but I also didn't want to be aggressive in my approach. I think I managed it, she looked intrigued when she spotted me.

"Who was he?" It was a dumb first question. I knew that before I started asking it. I could've introduced myself, I could've said literally anything else.

"My husband... I think?"

"I'm sorry." I sat down beside her, refusing to make eye contact even though she offered it freely. "I found him. There wasn't anything I could do."

"I don't remember him. Not properly, not in the way I should." She handed me a note. "It's not my handwriting but it was in my pocket. I'm assuming you're Violet. That would make as much sense as everything else going on."

Find us, Aeden Lynn and Violet DeCarter. 24hrs.

It was the unmistakable scrawl that had annoyed so many of my teachers growing up. "I am yeah. Do you know what's going on?"

She didn't. She told me her name, Alli, and filled me in as best she could. She explained to me what she knew, what she'd assumed, what she couldn't quite grasp. I offered her the same. We each filled in some of the blanks, she connected some of the dots I couldn't. Though not enough. Nowhere near enough.

The note was vague and that was clearly a point of frustration for her.

"Looks like I wrote it, maybe I didn't know it would work? A first try rather than a comprehensive catch up."

"I'd fill it with as much information as I could."

"I wouldn't. I don't know the rules, I don't know how this place works. I'd make it short and discrete, easy to hide, easy to overlook by whatever is roaming around out there."

"That makes sense, I guess." I watched the wheels turning in her brain. "And the pods all opened at midnight?"

"Except Marco. His opened roughly the same time Aeden might-" I didn't want to finish the sentence so I let myself get distracted. I realised I didn't know how long we'd been talking, I didn't know how long I'd been ignoring the gradually increasing static in my head.

"What's wrong?" As soon as I said the word static, she pulled me to my feet and pushed me into the cryo-pod.

She'd figured out the static meant danger was approaching, I was still unsure of the idea. I was unsure of everything going on. I trusted her, though. Far more than I should have. "Stay out of sight."

I heard her footsteps disappear down the row, most likely towards another empty pod. The static grew and grew, the vibrations in my head became almost unbearable. This time it didn't progress until I passed out, there was no screams. I felt scrambled but I stayed conscious.

The vibrations faded and I figured that meant it was safe, whatever was causing it had created enough distance between us. I peered out of the pod and was greeted by nothing. There was nothing crossing my path as I ventured out to find Alli.

I called out to her as I walked in the direction I thought she had gone. I didn't want to shout, I didn't want the static to come back, but loud enough for her to hear me as I got close. I heard a slight creak of a door and then she appeared from the next row over, slipping through the gap between two pods.

"It's gone." I wanted to sound reassuring but my voice cracked.

"My grandparents used to hunt." She started, quickly pausing to adjust her tone to something more light-hearted. "I was never fond of the practice but I never empathised with the fox as much as I did while waiting for that thing to go away."

"How often did the foxes escape?"

"I never asked. They weren't on a colony ship, though."

"You're right, they weren't. They didn't have escape pods. We do." I had the beginnings of a plan as I lead the way back to the computers.

I'd left him on the closest screen. I walked to a different computer, it felt respectful to leave him accessible to Alli. I didn't want to take that from her, and I didn't want to face him again. She sat with him while I looked up what I needed.

I'd found the escape pod symbol and the map very helpfully highlighted them all for me. Several of them were a concerning red colour.

I hesitated before I called her over, I wanted to offer her a little bit longer with her maybe-husband, but I finally had a plan and there was an urgency that I couldn't ignore.

"This is where we are." I pointed on the screen once she'd joined me. "And this is where we need to get to."

"What's wrong with these ones?" She pointed at a much closer, much redder, symbol.

"I feel like red is an error colour. Maybe they've been ejected already?" It was an optimistic idea, one neither of us countered.

We decided to plan our route past the one she'd pointed out, if they were available then we could take it, if not then at least we had a back-up plan. She found a tablet in one of the draws and copied the map over to it, highlighting the exact path we'd decided on.

We walked in silence. I wanted to talk. I desperately wanted some normalcy, a conversation where I could get to know the woman I'd just met, though maybe not for the first time. She smiled warmly, apologetically. I think she wanted the same, I hoped so at least, but she also wanted me to listen.

Her logic was sound but disappointing. The sooner I noticed the static, the safer we would be. Or, at least, the more time we would have to do something about it. Like pick a different route, one without static noises, or hide out in a cupboard for a bit because we didn't want to waste time trying out every door until we found something more comfortable.

Thankfully there weren't any close encounters on our journey, just some overly cautious detours and hiding places. We got to the closer escape pods as easily as we could have hoped for. A few of them had been ejected. A few of them had been destroyed.

Each pod had a door, each door had a window. The ejected ones had a shield replace the pod's door, the window just looked out onto a plain metal sheet. It was a surprisingly reassuring sight.

Over half of the windows looked out onto a mess of torn and melted metal. It looked like something had smashed through them. We only had an intermittent view of it, the windows were spaced out and didn't offer us any useful information, all we could do was speculate.

I suggested something crashed into us, she didn't seem too fond of the idea.

"The asteroid collision tech is top of the range, the route was planned to avoid them and then the tech was a well proven backup plan, it had a 99-point-whatever success rate."

"Maybe it wasn't an accident?"

"What, like, we were attacked?"

"We're an easy target. Sitting ducks for anyone who gets on board."

"No, they would have planned for that, this is the best technology around."

"Was. It was the best technology around. We don't know how long we've been asleep for, we can't know what progress has been made in that time."

"If we were targeted they would have just stripped the ship, taken whatever they wanted and gone, it would have been easy to get away."

"You're thinking pirates and profits, I'm thinking sport. We're being hunted. We're the foxes, like you said earlier."

"Whatever they are... will they let us leave?"

"Do you have a better plan?"

She shook her head. I didn't either so I focused on what we could do. I found the control panel. This one wasn't as convenient as the one for the pod's had been. This one was also far more broken, which definitely didn't help.

We were taught about how the escape-pods worked, when functional. A simple button press to open the door from the outside, a small space with 4 chairs, 2 at a computer screen and 2 behind. The computer had to be engaged to launch the pod. It was easy enough when working properly.

Some of the internal mechanisms must have been messed up alongside the missing escape-pods, none of the remaining ones had functional doors, not without some faffing, something we were running out of time to do. They opened, but they wouldn't close.

"We could try the others? The ones you suggested?"

I almost agreed. It would have been easier, but this was here and I was convinced it was fixable so I shook my head as the static through my hearing aid increased.

It was the right choice. I was convinced of that. I am still convinced of that. I don't regret it.

The control panel was convinced the escape-pod had been launched, so all we needed to do was reconnect it and then actually launch it. Between the both of us we had just enough experience to figure it out. We chose the pod furthest away from the destruction, it felt like that one had the highest chance of avoiding the worst of the damage, and then got to work.

I was already at the control panel so it was easy to convince her to go into the escape-pod. I explained what I thought needed doing, a reset vaguely similar to what my old hearing aid needed when the outdated tech decided to disengage from my implant, something it decided to do every few years. It wasn't exactly the same, of course, but it was close enough, and it was an experience I had that made me the expert between the two of us.

It almost worked. We managed to reconnect it, I could hear her celebrating, calling me over. I could just about hear her over the growing static. I knew what it meant. I didn't tell her. I couldn't tell her. I just slipped my hearing aid out and got on with saving her. It didn't fix the noise, the sensations, but it did give my body more time.

I couldn't fix the door. I could only close it manually. From the outside. There wasn't enough time to do that and hide. So I didn't. I just wished her luck and closed the door. I watched her turn to face me. I watched her realisation and then devastation. I watched the metal shield slam shut and she was gone and it was over

I didn't feel a thing.

BANISHED

Aria

It was always terrifying watching the guards storm around the island. Their presence was disconcerting, even when we knew the reason, even when we knew a member. Hayden, a friend of mine, was called to serve for a while, it was bizarre hating to see someone I loved so dearly. He said he didn't take it personally. I never believed him.

He was a good friend. He was there for it, though. He was the one who found me, who lead the process. I honestly don't know if that made it better or worse. He made it gentler, I'm certain of that. But the betrayal felt far more personal. He knew I hadn't done anything, but there was nothing he could do. There was nothing either of us could do, he was as helpless as I was, though obviously it was far worse for me.

We'd gone out to the local tavern to celebrate a birthday. It felt planned. He knew I'd be there with everyone. We'd planned it for weeks. We thought it was unfortunate he'd be on shift. I recommended postponing until we all were free, but it wasn't up to me. It wasn't my event. It wasn't my planning.

The birthday girl showed up just before the guards did, like moments before. We cheered her arrival until we saw her face. The sorrow, the fear, it was all right there. The cheers rapidly turned to worrying, to 'what's the matter?' and 'what's happened?'. And then the guards followed suit, pouring through the door and surrounding our little table. Surrounding me.

Hayden took charge. I assume he pulled some strings to do so. I dread to think what price he paid for it. He definitely didn't rank high enough for the task. He stepped forward, nonetheless.

He made eye contact, holding out his arm to beckon me forward. "Aria, I need you to come with us."

"Me?" I just barely squeaked out.

"Yes. Please don't make this any harder."

"I haven't done anything?" I stood up, only because I didn't know what else I could do.

"By high order of the Council, you are under arrest for treason."

"No. I haven't done anything."

"We have witnesses, Aria. You can't get out of this, please just come with me." He stepped forward again. He really must have made some good friends since this was usually the point it got violent. They were going easy on me. "You know how this goes."

I didn't have a choice. Not a good one, at least. He was right, I couldn't get out of this. I offered myself to him. I took the steps, followed him out of the tavern. There was no fight as I'd already lost the moment they decided to find me.

"Witnesses?" I asked meekly, surrounded by the guards.

"I'm not allowed to tell you. I've done as much as I can. I'm not risking anything more."

"Thank you."

He simply nodded and that was the end of it. That was the last conversation I had with anyone outside of the Council. The last conversation with anyone that cared about me. At least it was obvious he cared, obvious to everyone who understood. I don't know if you could understand.

He took a terrifying experience and made it as manageable as he could. It was still terrifying, but he did literally everything available to him and that mattered. It still matters to me. It kept me going far longer than it reasonably should have. It was all I had for a bit.

Nobody looked. Eyes were cast down, if you didn't look then you didn't have to see, if you didn't have to see then you didn't have to feel. Or at least, it made the attempt to not feel a whole lot easier. The dread would pass soon enough, the curiosity would creep in eventually, both would be manageable.

Eye contact makes it more real. It makes the person you're looking at more human, more familiar, more relatable. And then you have to live with that look once their fate has been decided. It's a lesson kids learn quickly. It's a lesson few adults have to re-experience. If you want to look, if the curiosity is too high, then you do it after the decision.

They walked me to the centre of town. It was a perfectly civil affair. I wasn't tied up, I wasn't beaten or dragged, I was allowed the dignity of walking to my execution. It definitely wasn't going to be imminent, and I didn't know for sure that's what was happening. It was the only assumption I could make, though.

He'd said treason. He'd said witnesses. I had no proof. I didn't even know what I had done. I did know nobody walked away from treason. Theft, assault, whatever other trivial things, you'd get community service or a little stay in the prison. Treason, there was only one punishment for that, and I was walking right to it.

The Council Manor stood proud in the centre of the square, around it was a ring of grass, a ring of road, and then the entire rest of the town. It was the biggest building on the island. It was also the grandest. No other building was decorated in such a way. It wasn't allowed.

And that's where they took me, that was where the death sentence was passed. I stood before the Council, stood in front of the brazier that lit me up and cast them in shadows. They sat above me, a ring of the most important people in our town. They were just vaguely humanoid figures that surrounded me.

Hayden told me to make sure I looked at whoever was speaking, to show them the reverence they deserved. I did, to start with. I did my best to follow the voices. The longer I stood in front of them the less human they became to me. They had no faces, no personalities, no morality. They were just entities that were judging me for a crime I didn't commit. They didn't deserve my reverence.

I stood before them and just stared into the fire. Once it became clear this was a game I couldn't win, a game I didn't know the rules of, I just stopped playing. It felt like my fate was already sealed, there wasn't anything I could do to change that. For better or for worse.

They talked, they deliberated, they made the exact same points over and over just phrased slightly differently each time. I don't think any of them actually told me what I'd supposedly done. I stopped listening after a while. There was nothing useful being said, just circle after circle until they settled on my punishment. It was treason. They didn't need to bother with all the show and tell, we all knew where it was leading.

Nobody called it a death sentence. It was 'banishment'. Everyone knew what that meant. You had to leave the island, you could only return with proof that you'd found other survivors, other settlements.

We knew there were other communities out there. People washed up on our shores every now and again, or bits of wreckage and cargo that got lost at sea. But knowing and finding were two very different things.

Banishment didn't happen very often, but nobody had ever come back from it. It was an imminent sentence, but the banishment wasn't.

They locked me in one of the Council Manor's rooms. I don't remember exactly how long I stayed there, however long it took to commission a rowboat, I guess. I was completely isolated from everyone, the only windows were sealed shut and no matter how much I tried to get a passerby's attention, no-one even glanced in my direction.

I was on the third floor, higher than I'd ever been, in a collection of rooms that were bigger than my house. I'd never experienced such luxury. I was given good food, a comfortable bed, clean and soft clothes whilst they washed mine, and a bath with delightfully warm running water.

It was supposed to be a slow death, a desperate one, thinly coated in mercy and compassion. I didn't know how else to view it. I'd always held hope for the people banished. I saw it as a merciful, though terrifying, punishment. Only now there was no hope, no real compassion. They made you look bad and made themselves look powerful. That's all it was, a power play.

They gifted you this luxury, they gifted you a rowboat. Oars and all. Even a makeshift shelter, though it was your responsibility to actually make that. One weeks' worth of dried food, two weeks' of clean water, a knife, a blanket. They had the means to do so.

They could have made up a decently sturdy and open-ocean based boat, they could have given supplies for multiple weeks, months even. They could have offered some of the finery to trade if a settlement was found. They had the resources.

All they offered was supposedly enough supplies to get you to the nearest land, though nobody knew where that was. I used to think the punishment was about redemption, about finding people, that the goal was for them to come back. It never was. It never could be. It was just wasting resources for a perverted torture that no one had to witness. And suddenly it was my turn.

The boat was ready, made to satisfaction, packed to regulation, and moored at the little inlet just outside the town edge. The tide was high, soon to turn. It was early morning, everyone who wanted to watch were ready and waiting.

The guards paraded me through the town. Once again there was no eye contact, but everyone watched. I didn't see any of my friends, not until I reached the boat. Hayden was stood there, off duty so just a part of the crowd.

Mostly it was just youngsters who had showed up, those who had never experienced a banishing before, and whatever adult they'd managed to talk into accompanying them.

I recognised most of them, though only in passing. Hayden was the only one there I knew with any familiarity, and he wasn't allowed to say anything to me. He did look though, the entire time, he offered me the dignity of looking at me like I was a human. He looked so heartbroken I could barely return his gaze. But I did, I had to.

He was the last point of humanity I had access to. The last remnant of caring compassion. He was a lifeline I was going to lose within a matter of minutes. Once I was in that boat, I couldn't focus on anything beyond surviving. If surviving was my goal.

I'd had a lot of time to think about it. I'd thought through the best-case scenarios, the worst-case scenarios, the realistic scenarios. My definition of best-case got a little skewered. It didn't take long for me to conclude that a quick death was far better than a slow one and a slow one was far more realistic unless I took matters into my own hands.

I'd settled on the idea. I'd planned it out. I knew I wouldn't be able to do anything with an audience that could intervene, but once the tide had taken me out far enough... Well, I could get away with whatever. It wouldn't matter to anyone. They gifted me a knife I could... It was so easy to think about, to just... I could just...

I couldn't.

I'd toyed with the idea before, even when things were normal, and I just never could. I expected this to be different. It was different, but that didn't change anything.

Meeting Hayden's gaze was a point of no return. I was loved, I was cared for, I had at least one good friend who did everything he could for me when I was at my worst. I wasn't going to waste his efforts.

He had done more for me than I could ever know so I returned the favour, I did more for him than he could ever know. And he would never know. Whether I lived or died, he would never know. There was just an assumption that those who were banished died, and that's what I was leaving him with, what I was leaving them all with.

It was a weird head space to be in. A lot was happening within a very short walk down that beach. It could only have been a few minutes between reaching the inlet and stepping foot on that boat but so much had changed in that time. My original resolve had vanished, replaced with something far less convenient.

I went from fear and uncertainty to survival. Something desperate and primal. I can't say I was unfamiliar with the feeling, but it hadn't been so obvious before. That survival kept me walking, it kept me upright and functional, like it had so many times before. It got me to the edge of the water, ankle deep, up to my calves, and then my knees.

Two guards stood holding the boat in place as the rippling waves splashed up their thighs. Soon enough I was stood beside them. A third offered me her arm to help stabilise me as I stepped aboard and settled down. Between them, they pushed my tiny little vessel out until the tide caught it, pulling me away from my home.

I'd been alone for a while, but never this alone. Watching everything I'd ever known slowly get further and further away. I felt everything I needed to for a while. I sobbed, I toyed with the knife a little more, I played out every scenario I'd thought up since my arrest, and then I got to work.

Wet feet was a dreadful way to start a journey. I removed as much of my wet clothing as I comfortably could and laid it out in what little space I had. The sun was still low, it hadn't had a chance to warm up yet, but there was plenty of time for it all to dry as the sun and temperature both rose.

Shelter was my next priority. They'd provided a well-oiled cloth, decent size, some sturdy sticks to use as supports, and an abundance of rope. It briefly crossed my mind that I could probably make a sail out of it, but the sky was far too clear to entertain that idea. Creating shade was more important.

It took me a few tries to rig up something I was content with, but I managed it without too much faff. A few curses, perhaps, but it was relatively secure and even somewhat adjustable. That seemed easier than having to plan for where the sun would be at its worst.

The cloth was more or less centred, high enough for me to sit under. I could move with the shade, lower a particular side if I needed, or even both if I was worried about the weather. I didn't know if my logic actually made sense, but I found reassurance in it, nonetheless.

It was a good start, if nothing else.

Food and water was my next concern. They'd fed me well at the Manor, so it wasn't a concern I needed to rush, and I had a reasonable supply.

I didn't know how long I'd be out there for, I didn't know how to best ration it all. I could be hungry for a bit, I'd had some experience with that, but water was going to be challenging.

I didn't know how long I could go without water. I figured probably not long. I'd never had a chance to experiment with that one, I'd never needed to. I also didn't have the resources to purify my own supply of water. I had, however, seen the effect of long-term dehydration. I knew I had to avoid that.

Another issue was strength. I had none. Or, at least, very little. Not enough to make the oars particularly efficient, especially as I had no compass, no concept of directions, no way of knowing if I was going in a useful direction. There was no point in rowing if I ended up going in circles by accident, especially with limited food, water, and energy.

I decided to treat it as an activity to keep me occupied, as opposed to anything useful. As pointless as it felt, sitting there doing nothing felt worse. The movement of my body was something I could use as a distraction. I didn't need to think when my muscles were working.

It felt like rowing required a direction to aim for, but I was aimless, so there was no point in aiming. I tried to see the freedom in that, in not needing to care about the specifics, but there was too much anxiety in that uncertainty, and that was not beneficial to me. Thinking wasn't beneficial.

There was also no point in tracking time. I didn't care to think about it. Days and nights passed, and I simply floated through them all. I ate when I was hungry, drank when I was thirsty, slept when I was tired, rowed when I was bored. I knew not to be stupid about any of it. I didn't see any point in limiting myself, either.

Death was inevitably going to be closer to me than life was until land came into view. And I was far from convinced that that was even something that could happen. There was too much open water. There was only open water. Flat, endless, nothingness.

There was one morning when I woke up and everything was so still. There wasn't a hint of a breeze, I swear even my little boat was stationary. The current had done a great job at keeping me moving until that point. I had to assume it was moving me and I was only imagining that eery stagnation. I had no way of knowing.

There was no point of reference, nothing to compare my movement to. I just felt bizarre. I must have become used to the constant sway, all the micro-adjustments needed to keep my balance, to keep comfortable or even in the boat. It was nauseating expecting movement that wasn't there. I got more rowing done during that time than I did any other day.

Honestly, I got pretty lucky. For the most part, the weather stayed easy. The stagnation was disconcerting, but it wasn't scary, and I was convinced it was all in my head. The first scary thing I encountered was the wildlife. Up close and personal.

I think the shark was the scariest. I didn't see what it caught, but I did witness a whole lot of splashing and the horrendous red patch it left in its wake, I drifted through it once the commotion had settled down. There was plenty of distance between me and the action, I wasn't in any danger, but the anxiety it caused lingered.

I couldn't shake the idea of it nudging me, of it knocking my little boat over. I was an easy meal and all I could do was hope it didn't know I was there. I'd almost convinced myself there was no way anything could know about my presence, that's when I met some delightfully curious whales.

I'd never really realised how big they were before. I'd never been next to one. Some of the fishermen had, but they were prone to exaggeration so you couldn't believe exactly what they said. A general rule was to half any estimate they made. In this case it was fairly safe to double it.

I wasn't really paying attention around me, I was making stories in the clouds, or something stupid like that. At some point a humming noise had started up, vibrations that were felt more than heard.

It took me some time to notice it, to draw me out of my reverie. And obviously I met it with confusion, I thought I was just imagining things again, maybe I'd been in the sun for too long or the madness of isolation was creeping its way in.

It was only when the waves changed their pattern, when I looked over the edge of the boat, only once I noticed an eye staring at me did I understand what was happening. And even then I could hardly believe it.

The fishermen called them humpbacks, the descriptions matched what I saw but I couldn't know for sure that they were the same.

They were incredible. Truly stunning. One of them surfaced right next to me.

It met my gaze with such humanity, such intelligence. I never knew animals were capable of such a thing. It wasn't my equal, it was so much more. This beautiful creature had more experience than I was capable of understanding, it had access to a world I couldn't possibly fathom. I wasn't religious but that moment was the closest I'd ever got to meeting God.

Nothing really existed on the open ocean. I certainly didn't. The whales were a turning point. I was thrown back into a humanity I didn't know I'd lost. Death wasn't just around the corner anymore, there was life. And far more of it than I was prepared for.

They stayed with me for some time. Not quite as close, and not particularly consistently, but every time I thought they'd left I'd catch sight of a tail or a spurt of water.

Their company was invaluable. It helped ground me in the moment, remind me I wasn't just a vague concept-less being like my brain had become prone to believing.

It was great while it lasted. They couldn't stay forever. I knew that but it was still sad realising they probably weren't coming back.

The seas had started to churn in a way that filled me with anxiety. It was a slow change, one I missed most of because I was so caught up in the whales. I missed the opportunity to plan properly. Even if I could have, I don't think I would have known what to factor in, instead I went with instinct.

I secured everything as best I could, not that I had much left at that point. As soon as I noticed the ominous clouds, I did what I could to steer away from them. It was the only time I felt like I had a direction.

Just, away. No navigating required. It was more than I'd had in weeks and frankly it was awful. I started rowing whilst the sea was choppy. It was uncomfortable and exhausting.

The waves gradually progressed from manageable, to choppy, to large and slightly terrifying. I knew rain was coming, I could see it on the horizon. I could see it racing towards me.

I couldn't outrun a storm. I got to the point where could barely stay upright with the rising and falling waves. I was riding hills of water that were gradually getting steeper and steeper, bigger and bigger, faster and faster.

The rains hit hard. My attempts to row had long since been futile, but I'd kept it up out of some sort of need to do something, anything, to keep myself going. The rains gave me something else to focus on as the water in my boat started to climb. I ditched the oars, they weren't of use to me anymore.

I had nothing to bail the water out of my boat with. There was so much from the sky and the waves, just going everywhere, in and out of my boat with no real pattern I could make sense of.

What was left of my resources was soon swept overboard as it all shifted with the water in my boat and the waters driving my boat. Between desperately splashing the water out of my vessel and hanging on for dear life, I grabbed what little I could and shoved it down my shirt for safekeeping.

And then came the winds and there was nothing I could do. I was being battered from all around me, everything I did was futile. I couldn't let go of my boat, for risk of falling in. I knew if I fell then that was it, there was no surviving that.

I knew that with so much certainty, it was the kind of knowledge you feel deep in your bones. My boat was being tossed around so much, there was no way I could choose what happened to me, so I held on. That was all I could do, up until I couldn't anymore.

I felt myself thrown through the air. I was soaked through, I felt so heavy, so tired, and then I was just falling. My boat had been damn near upside down at that point.

I just gave up. It was terrifying. It was hopeless. Everything was so loud. I was alone and falling and crashing and sinking and it was the last thing I could do. I gave up.

I let my body go whatever way it ended up going. The water took me wherever it wanted. I rose up with the waves and I fell back down with them. I tossed and turned against my will and I gasped for breath any time my face touched air. I held my breath anytime I felt myself submerged. None of it was choices. I had no control over my body.

Finally, I went under and I didn't come up in time. I couldn't fight instincts and my lungs were desperate. Instead of air, they met water and that was it. Everything closed in around me and I couldn't stay conscious.

I don't know what happened next. Other than a string of incredibly lucky circumstances. They told me about it afterwards, once we'd reached gentler waters.

All I knew was that it felt like I coughed up half the ocean. My entire body hurt, bruises and muscle spasms and lingering droplets in my chest. I couldn't focus my eyes, so I kept them shut. I couldn't think at all, so I didn't.

On the edge of my hearing was a soft voice. I couldn't understand what he was saying. It was just jumbled nonsense, another language. I only realised that once I'd recovered.

He kept talking to me, I did try to look at him, to make eye contact, but everything was too blurry, too painful, to bother with for long.

He must have noticed, his speech turned from soft and soothing into something more insistent. It almost sounded like questions.

He gently tapped my cheek and I opened my eyes again, it was the only way I knew how to acknowledge him. It spurred him on but there was no understanding.

He placed his hand in mine and gave it a squeeze. I returned the gesture and he immediately lifted me up, carrying me across the deck and onto something soft and that was it for a while.

I don't know how long I slept for. I dipped in and out of

awareness for what felt like an age. I think it was the same guy who bought me food and drink, who'd found me, who'd saved me, who'd forced as much water out of my body as he could.

He left a handprint around my arm, where he'd grabbed me and pulled me aboard. Somehow, I'd got within reaching distance of a merchant ship. Somehow, he'd spotted me, he'd looked in the exact right direction at the exact right moment and reacted instantly. Luck after luck.

There were a few men aboard who spoke a similar language as I did, there were some differences, but we figured out enough to have a conversation. They each stepped up when need but one in particular did the brunt of it.

He did his best to explain their side of the situation, where they were going, and roughly how far we were from their destination. About 2 weeks until they'd reach their homeland, he told me, if things went smoothly.

In that time, once I was better, he taught me the basics of their common language. Things like how to ask for food or water, the bare minimum to give me some form of agency. I got introduced to whoever was around, in turn I introduced myself.

I was invited to share my story, with help with translations, and I was shown so much empathy and compassion. These men met me, listened to me, cared for me as best they could. They offered me help, companionship, they included me when it was safe to do so and made sure I was secured away when it wasn't.

This was community. Not based on fear and survival, despite the numerous reasons to fear and the constant threat of death. They sang, they chatted and laughed and there was so often an air of joviality. Things I thought had to be reserved for special occasions were such common place amongst these people. It was incredible.

At first, I was worried about what they were saying, I had no way of knowing if they were talking about me, or in what way they were talking about me, but I got past that far quicker than I ever thought possible.

I started picking up on some phrases, just the easy ones. The man translating for me offered some jokes so I could join in, ones he knew would go down well.

Sometimes someone would approach me and then stumble their way through something in my language. An offer to include me in some way, to show me some knots or ask for a hand cooking, simple tasks I could reasonably do.

They even taught me to dance.

On a soft evening, a calm sea and colourful sky, they took time out of their rest to show me what to do. Some sang, some watched, some joined in. They joked and guided and celebrated with me.

They were perfect gentlemen. Consistently whilst I was there, I was shown nothing but respect. No wandering hands, no roughness. These men were nothing like the ones back home. If someone crossed a line, someone else spoke up, even when I had no way of knowing there had been an issue. I never had to defend myself.

And then I spotted a bird, the first one, a sign that we were nearing shore, someone explained after the cheers died down. It landed on the mast and one of the men climbed up to offer it some fish. For good luck, they explained.

A call of land soon followed, though it took a while before I could see it. A small slither on the horizon and so much relief.

I thought I was subtle, I was looking away from everyone and being quiet, but then a hand settled on my shoulder, and I couldn't contain it. The guy who'd pulled me out of the sea, Teku was his name, he pulled me into a hug as I cried. He'd been one of the more enthusiastic to include me, to support me. He'd become a friend despite initially not sharing any language.

He offered me comfort as best he could for as long as he could, as we neared the land the amount of work needed seemed to pick up. Everyone was getting excited and rushing around, doing all the checks they needed. I just put myself as far out of the way as I could and watched them, watched our progress.

Soon the port came into view, from a distance it looked almost as big as the entire island I'd left behind. Busier by far. It was intimidating to see.

Someone explained that this wasn't their home, they had cargo to drop off, a few of the men would leave as well, before moving around the coast to their home. Another day or so of travelling.

I was given the option to leave if I wanted, I wasn't ready to. These were the only people I knew and I had no desire to abandon them yet. I certainly didn't have the resources.

I was strongly encouraged to stick with them. I was offered a place to stay, they'd figure something out amongst themselves. Someone would have a spare room, they were sure.

Their town would welcome me in, they promised. I believed them. I absolutely took them up on that offer. It was the best option available to me.

Like I said, I got pretty lucky. I found land, I'd found people who were willing to help me, and I was never going back to that godforsaken island I used to call home.

MR & MRS ADAIR

Camille

It was a day like any other, the sun rose in the east, the birds called in the early morning, and my body lay across their front lawn.

Ok, so, perhaps it wasn't like any other, for this exact morning hadn't happened in at least a few months. In fact, their last body mishap had occurred in the middle of winter and it had since become the tail end of spring. Practically summer, even.

"My love?" Mr Adair called out to his wife. "Do you know who our guest is?"

Mrs Adair meandered over to him before peering out of their window. "Feels like one of the Bardot's. That's unfortunate, they're a lovely bunch."

"The bakers?"

"Uh-huh."

"Perfect, I'll pick up a loaf while you try and find the poor dear."

"After coffee?"

"After coffee."

She popped the kettle on the fire while he settled down with his newspaper. There was no rush since the bakery didn't open for a couple of hours and it was widely regarded as rude to bother people at such times.

There was, also, the ritual to prepare. That was Mrs Adair's domain. Mr Adair had never been particularly comfortable getting his hands dirty, so to speak. He was more of a people person.

I don't know how I knew any of that. I'd never met those people before.

I found myself in the weird position of just knowing things. I looked and I knew. Understanding was a whole other issue, though. I definitely didn't understand any of what was happening. I also didn't understand where I was.

I wasn't in my body, that much was obvious. My body was over on their lawn and I definitely wasn't. I wasn't really anything, I was just around. It's not an experience I'd recommend. It wasn't unpleasant, just bizarre.

I could access everything and nothing, all at once and never at all. I was everywhere and nowhere. Everywhere is an exaggeration, I was very much limited to the Adair's property boundary, which honestly kind of made it harder to comprehend. There was a wrongness to that limitation that I couldn't even begin to comprehend.

I shouldn't have been there. Not in some denial, why me, kind of way. Like genuinely, my existence in that middle ground should not have been possible. And yet there I was, there my body lay, and there was the old couple who were distinctly unphased by the whole situation.

Neither of them were in any rush. I couldn't blame them, I was an intrusion on their morning, after all. A little urgency would have been appreciated, though

Mr Adair placed his paper down with a flourish, something he'd perfected many years previously. He finished the last sip of his coffee and then gently pushed himself out of his chair and towards his wife.

"I'd best be off." He gave her a soft peck on the forehead and made his way to the door. He was outside of my awareness a few minutes later.

"Deary, we were thoroughly unprepared for your visit this morning, I'm going to have to ask you to be patient while I get everything ready. I am sorry for the inconvenience of it all, I can't begin to imagine how you're feeling."

I knew she was talking to me because it was one of the things I knew. Not because it made sense, or any kind of logic. It was just instant knowledge.

Once she was ready, she made her way through to the back room. An apothecary with a delightful collection of herbs and other such ingredients. Most were stored appropriately, in little jars and boxes and envelopes, some hanging from the ceiling, drying in pretty brunches.

There were also little piles of assorted plants littering the workspace, waste product she didn't need anymore. She promptly brushed them onto the floor and then out the door into the garden, throwing out what remained in her mortar as she did so.

"What's your name, love?" She asked as she rummaged around.

Camille.

I didn't know how I was supposed to respond. I couldn't talk, I couldn't interact, she was thoroughly cut off from me. All I could do was think it at her.

"Camille," she chuckled to herself, "perhaps some chamomile is in order then."

She reached up to one of the hanging bunches and picked off a few flower heads.

"Our last visitor wasn't interested in flowers, which was fair enough of course. I would never judge for such a thing, but I can't deny it felt odd. I couldn't shake the feeling something was missing, but it all worked fine so maybe I was just being a little dramatic. Letting my own floral fixation get the better of me."

She talked me through every step, picking and choosing the exact pieces she wanted to use before throwing them in the mortar and working them with the pestle. I watched as she ground up her ingredients into an impressively fine dust. It was all very precise.

"Shan't be long now, dear." She said as she finally put down the pestle. "I think that's all I need from here. This bit is a little gross and I'm sorry."

She decanted the dust into a little bowl and then spat into it. With a little stir, the brown mixture shifted into a bright red hue and Mrs Adair smiled in delight.

"Perfect. This should be a breeze." She made her way back out to the lawn where I lay, placing the bowl next to my body. "Join in please, love. I'm sure you can know the words."

She was right, I could. I matched her word for word as she walked a circle around me, knelt beside me, and drew symbols on my body. Feet, hands, heart, and forehead. I felt every symbol drawn on me, each stronger and more physical than the last.

By the time she was drawing on my forehead, I was right there beneath her hand, watching her through my eyes. She met my gaze as she finished up and then sat down on the grass.

"Hello dear. How are you feeling?"

"I..." My voice was hoarse and strained, but it was my voice, from my body.

"Perhaps some water is in order?"

I nodded. That was a thing I could do again. My head lifted up and back down. It was a weird sensation. It all was.

I'd lost so much, having access to everything and then nothing. It was devastating and relieving. I'd got my normality back, but at such a cost. How do you go from feeling everything around you, understanding everything, knowing everything, back into something so limiting as the human body?

All I could do was stand up and follow her back into the house. I accepted the water and replenished myself, something I hadn't needed only minutes beforehand. I sat down and I drank and I felt it filling my body up in such an unpleasant way. I was everything and then suddenly water was overwhelming.

I had to navigate the physical, move my body in a way that matched my surroundings. There was so much to think about all of the time. I couldn't just *be* anymore. I had to think and plan and make my own sense of things. How do you do that? How do you go back to such a small existence?

Mr Adair returned whilst I was caught up in my thoughts. I didn't know he was there until he was stood in front me. Even then, I nearly didn't notice. He greeted me pleasantly, loaf under arm and my mother in tow.

"How are you feeling?" He asked gently. I just stared.

"The acclimatising can be rough, sometimes." Mrs Adair filled in. "I think it's hitting her harder than most."

I nodded.

My mother lingered in the background. She held her hands over chest, clasped together in the way she always did when she was worried.

"What do I need to do?" She asked quietly.

"Take your daughter home. Get her cleaned up and give her some time. She wasn't supposed to die, that's why she's here, but nobody goes through that unscathed. There'll be a cost. Support her through it." Mr Adair responded. He was firm but not demanding. He responded exactly as she needed.

"I died?" I forced the words out. I knew they were true, it was one of the first things I had truly known. But I was small again and those words were ever so heavy.

"Yes." No sugar coating. No lies to appease. A simple answer. "You'll forget over the next few days, forget most of this. It'll get easier, I promise."

My mother helped me to my feet. She linked arms with me and led me to the door and down the garden pathway. The couple followed and watched from the threshold.

"Come back if you need anything, love. We can always help." Mrs Adair called out just before we left view.

I was supposed to forget.

I didn't forget.

I never saw them again.

THE END OF YOUR NEW LIFE

You woke up that morning, waiting for your life to change, hoping that that was the day. You did that a lot, but finally it was. Your life changed. You went above and beyond. We gave you a job and you've done it wonderfully.

You were missed and that makes us sad. You had so much more potential than any of them could ever have seen. You didn't have the opportunities. We gave you the opportunity. You didn't have a chance to shine and now here you are, stepping into your light. And it makes us sad that they couldn't see it like we can. We're not used to feeling this.

We're breaking protocol again. Last time was worth the reprimand and we hope this time is as well.

You took this job, you took this step, you took something scary and overwhelming and you made it into an adventure. You took the opportunity and you made it yours.

We've seen so many people go through this process. So many people try and fail, so many scraping by, and only a few thrive. You are thriving. You are a product of your stories, of your collection. Most people can't handle that much, and you've only just begun. You have the universe at your fingertips and all you need to do is reach out. You've proved your capability.

This is the end of your new life. It's not new any more. This is your life now.

AFTERWORD

Thank you for reading my work and supporting me on this endeavour.

This is my first self published book and it has been a wonderful experience and massive step towards fulfilling a childhood dream. I am ever so proud of myself and of the work I have done here.

I have previously had a story included in an anthology, The Cream of Devon, and hopefully soon I will have even more of my work out in the world.

Printed in Great Britain
by Amazon